THE ORC OUTCAST'S CONQUEST

ORC MATES OF FAEDA

BOOK ONE

AURORA WINTERS

ISBN: 978-1-963552-01-0

CONTENT WARNINGS

All content warnings can be viewed on Aurora Winters's website at www.AuroraWintersRomance.com.

CHAPTER
ONE

MIRANDA

Miranda chewed her parched tongue, willing saliva to form, and only made her mouth taste like gritty sand. Her fingers trembled and her feet slid against the dry ground, toes skidding in shoes a size too big for her.

The sound echoed off the hillside, which was barren except for the haunting remains of crisp black trees. Their needles and branches were burned away, leaving nothing but jutting, pointed trunks that pierced threateningly at the cloudless sky. They surrounded her completely, looming ahead, flanking the road she was walking on until they swallowed it up in the distance.

Just days ago, this was a beautiful forest, with green pine trees and soft patches of moss and birds flying overhead. She loved driving this road to the coast, rolling down her windows to breathe in the scent of warm wood and ocean salt.

It was all gone. Everything was *gone*.

She squeezed her eyes shut, agony rippling through her chest. She took deep, burning breaths and turned the rising pain into determination. She wiped her dry hands on the workout shorts she'd stolen, a nervous tick, and dug the string straps of her bag into her almost bare shoulder. The sun beat down on her, relentless. Her mind was about as melted as the mile marker sign she was staring down, all warped and confused.

This was the third sign she'd passed this morning. They were becoming more frequent. The first day, when she'd started walking out of the rubble that had once been her hometown, she'd only passed five. She'd been so numb then. So lost and unfocused. She'd seen the milepost marker all lit up in the growing dim of sunset, *"Pacific Ocean, 42 miles ahead,"* and she'd followed it blindly because *someone* must have gotten them working right? A survivor must have left them for others to find.

But she'd seen not a soul since. At least not a *human* soul.

Now, three days later she'd counted a total of twenty-seven during her trek across the blistering, barren landscape. A path she followed on pure instinct alone. Driven by nothing more than her own gut screaming that the ocean was the answer.

It is. Keep going.

Miranda squeezed her eyes shut and took a long deep breath into her burning lungs. She had to get out of here. She had to keep following the signs even if they didn't make any sense. Everything had been burnt to a crisp and yet these electronic milepost markers still worked. How was that possible? There was something strange about it. Something inconceivable that pricked the corners of her ragged senses.

Just keep going.

So, she did. She pushed forward past her own sanity. Even as her mind was shattering, and the sorrow was sucking her down and bone deep dread swelled so high she couldn't breathe. She pressed on. Following these strange, miraculous signs that blazed her trail.

Her feet kept a steady gait even as the crumbling highway under them grew steep. But steep was good. Steep meant she would get to the lookout soon.

One mile to the ocean.

One mile was *nothing*. She'd walked through utter destruction. New Seattle was completely leveled.

The highway was rubble and all the cars she passed were burned out except for a select few. A few that only showed up when she was at her lowest. When her muscles were cramping from fatigue and her mouth was so dry it felt like ash and her stomach was burning itself up in a pit of acid.

Those miraculous cars that shouldn't have been there always had food, and water. They gave her the will to keep going even as she considered they might be a mirage. A delusion conjured up by her own desperation.

She hadn't passed one since midday the day prior and her eyes scanned desperately. Dusty ground, cracked pavement, burnt trees. Not a single miracle car in sight.

She was starting to reach the edge of her endurance again.

But it was just *one mile*.

She squeezed her eyes shut so tight that light burst behind her eyelids, drowning out the horrible image of the city she'd lived in in utter *ruin.*

Forty-one miles she'd trudged with determination raging in her. Three blistering days and freezing nights. She'd worked her way across chaotic rubble, raided vehicles that were inexplicably untouched, and scraped together just enough supplies to stay alive.

She didn't want to die.

She was so dang *close.*

She wasn't going to die.

One mile.

She should be hurt. Bruised. Broken. Laying in the wastes.

But she wasn't. And she wouldn't. She would not give up.

God, she was thirsty.

Miranda gave into the urge to dig through her pack again even though she knew there was nothing left. She'd drank all the bottled water and eaten her last bite of granola bar the day before.

Still, she swung the pack to her front, not breaking her stride. She had to outrun the radiation. Fallout from By-Pass nuclear bombs would be spreading behind her. She had to keep moving. Stay ahead of it.

Miranda looked down at her arm. Fingered the little pricks where she'd given herself the radiation boosters. She'd found them tucked away under the front seat of the first car she'd raided with crisp clear instructions on how to use them printed along the side of the canister. Not that she didn't remember. Almost every American had these boosters tucked away in their homes and cars. She still remembered most of the "Fallout preparedness" videos they'd watched almost weekly in high school.

Humans had been preparing for this eventuality for her entire lifetime, but she never thought she would actually have to live through it. That she would be the lone survivor.

She wasn't the only survivor. She couldn't be. They *would* be at the ocean.

Miranda went back to searching her bag. The drawstring pack was flimsy. The kind that people gave out for free at fairs. It displayed the logo for a company in crisp white on the blue front, three lines with a stylized mountain in the background. Or maybe it was supposed to be a treadmill? She found it with the gym clothes she was wearing.

It didn't matter. She'd found it, and it was hers. Just like the workout clothes and the shoes and the water bottle and the granola bars. She had to leave everything behind, and now she wore a stranger's trim black gym shorts, sports bra, and tank top. Because it was clean, and it fit, and her own clothes were irradiated.

Her clothes had been at the epicenter of the bombs. *She had been* at the epicenter of the bombs. She'd heard them go off above her. Seen the charred remains of New Seattle. Nothing could have survived.

She shouldn't have either. She should be irradiated too. Might still be. The boosters might not be enough.

Miranda's fingers clenched around the empty water bottle. The cheap plastic crinkled under her fingers, giving way with little pops. Such an odd sound in the eerie silence.

Nothing made *any* sense. Everything else was destroyed. *Everything.*

Keep going.

Miranda shook her head, cleared her mind, listened for

threats, the scampering of feet, the fluttering of birds taking flight. Her ears were ringing in the deadly silence. She wanted to say something aloud just to rid herself of the pain, but her throat throbbed, and her teeth were sticky.

And was it worth the risk that the dogs might find her again?

Those damn dogs. She'd only seen them once on that first day, but it had been more than enough.

They'd chased her for what felt like an eternity. Driving her to move even when all she wanted to do was collapse. Forcing her to forget everything she had lost. Making her put the city she'd been born and raised in behind her and look only forward. Toward the road signs.

The road signs that shouldn't be working.

Her head blazed with agony as she raked through her thoughts.

How had she survived the blast? How had she escaped the rubble? How had she made it this far?

How was *any* of this possible?

Don't think about it.

Miranda breathed deep as her heart raced, and her palms sweat, and her mind began to fracture under the weight of those horrific first moments after the bombs hit. When she was trapped underground. The crunching of metal. The horrible heat.

Stop. There's no time.

She didn't have time to fall apart here.

She had to get to the ocean.

There would be people at the ocean. Why would they bother lighting up the mile marker signs if they weren't gathering at the ocean? And a bunch of people would *surely* be there, right? There would be boats and planes and emergency services.

Right?

Someone *was* lighting up these signs.

No. Not just *someone*.

She would make it to the base camp and search the crowd for their faces, strain her ears over the symphony of voices. Their eyes would meet despite the chaos.

Taylor. Or Josephine. Or Robby. Or any one of the other toddlers she looked after during her shifts at Riverside Daycare.

Her babies.

They would be there, right? They had to be. Maybe their parents or her co-workers were the ones lighting up these signs.

No. Not maybe. *Definitely.*

Her babies and the people who saved them had *definitely* been the ones to get these road signs working. They were the ones guiding her this way. *They were.*

She hadn't gone back for them, but *someone* had. Someone must have saved them. *Surely they had.*

Miranda's stomach heaved, her eyes burned, and her body shook under the relentless weight crushing around her heart.

She should have been there. She should have been there that day to save them. She shouldn't have taken that job at the bank, no matter how good the pay was. No matter how nice her new boss was. No matter how badly she needed more stable hours so she could eventually get a promotion and quit the night shifts at the daycare and finally—*finally!*—be able to adopt children of her own.

She'd left them. All those little ones she loved so much.

She'd been selfish and abandoned them, and now they were—

Breathe. Calm.

Miranda forced a shaky breath. If she fell apart here, if she let herself succumb to the agony growing in her chest, she would not have the strength to get back up.

She would never see them again.

They hadn't been at the daycare when the bombs dropped. She knew it. Parents always had a sixth sense about these things. They would have woken up with an odd tingling in their stomach or a burning at the back of their mind. They would have squeezed their little ones tight and called the daycare and told them their babies would be absent that day and they would have gotten to a bomb shelter in time and now they were hiking across the desolation, like her. Just like Miranda was now.

They would meet at the ocean.

And then they would all get on the boat together. Traveling to their new home somewhere nuclear bombs couldn't reach. She'd hold those babies close, watch them so their parents could get some much-needed sleep. Warm little bodies all snuggled up. Soak up their life. They were alive.

So was she.

Her eyes prickled with tears as she slung her bag back over her shoulder, and turned her gaze upward, toward the endless blue sky.

"Five things I can see," Miranda mouthed, careful not to make a sound because *the dogs*. Her lips were cracking, her tongue was sticking, and she ignored it as she began her usual exercise for soothing anxiety.

Miranda doubted the inventor had thought it might be useful for someone who'd survived the apocalypse.

"Stumps," she exhaled slowly, eyes falling to the landscape once more as she picked up the pace again. "Five black stumps." There were well over five. There were hundreds. Thousands. She couldn't see anything else. She was supposed to be in the national park nestled between the city and the sea, but it was a burned black waste now.

Four things she could feel. "The back of my shoe scraping my heel, the hard pavement, the scorching sun, and my sandy tongue." There was no wind. No movement of air other than what her own steady pace provided. It was like the bombs had wiped out the breeze along with everything else.

"Three things I can hear," she shivered, hugged herself, and pressed her hands together. "My breathing, my steps, and my heart." She didn't want to think about what she *couldn't* hear. The ocean was still too far away. The crashing waves and rumble of the survivors' voices wouldn't reach her until she was at the top.

Miranda sniffed quickly, cutting off the inhale as her nose burned. "Bleach. All I can smell is bleach."

Better than a lot of other things. She'd found the bleach citrus spray in the second car. Right after the one where she found her pilfered clothes. She knew the pungent scent of chlorine would hide her scent and throw the dogs off her trail. Those horrible mangy beasts who howled every night and haunted every scrap of her waking hours.

Just keep going.

"One to taste." She almost laughed at her folly. She didn't want to focus on her mouth's muddy grit. What would she do for a gulp of clean water? A bite of a cheeseburger? What *wouldn't* she do?

In desperation, Miranda pulled her bag forward and dug around. Her hand closed around the last item she had with any liquid in it.

A bingo dauber. The kind you used on actual *paper*.

She'd found it in the glove compartment of one of those really old electric vehicles. The ones that actually had a push button start instead of a fingerprint or retina scanner.

She tried to imagine what sort of back-alley biddy had used it. Someone with enough nerve to risk getting caught with illegal paper, which had been banned from production five years before—another desperate attempt to save their world's natural resources before it was too late.

Like it had mattered. Like *paper* had been what was killing Earth and not constant corporate pollution and countries sparking up new resource wars. Wars that dropped deadly bombs and turned once glorious national parks, like the one surrounding her now, into burned husks.

Stop. Keep going.

Miranda pushed herself onward. Sloshing the ink in the dauber's canister. Wondering if she should drink it.

As she thought, she let her mind wander back to a memory at the daycare, a day when Susan, the director, had scrounged up a bucket of blackberries. They'd mashed, strained, and diluted them with vinegar. Then they divided the makeshift ink out to all the kids. Letting them paint with it on a white tablecloth.

They'd splattered their little purple handprints all over it. The laughter sang in Miranda's mind and her chest loosened.

It made her smile even now. Despite everything.

A crack sounded behind her. The snap of a branch.

She knew before she looked.

The dogs.

Calling them dogs was a kindness. They were heaving, massive, black mangy beasts with endless teeth and drooling mouths. Their ears were slicked back, their fangs dripped with saliva, and their chests rumbled with menacing growls. Their stench, rotting flesh and sour vomit bubbling in the unending sun, punctuated Miranda's nostrils over the bleach.

Somehow, despite all she had done, they had tracked her.

And she hadn't seen them coming.

It should have brought her some comfort to see another living creature. Instead, as her eyes landed on the three monsters stalking her, she felt only the icy lump of dread.

The one in the front snapped, snarled, and stepped forward.

Fear exploded into action, and she whirled away. Feet scrambling on the dry ground as she burst into a sprint. She knew she shouldn't run. It would only make them chase her. But she was stupid and panicked.

Miranda bolted, realized she was so much closer to the viewpoint overlooking the ocean than she'd realized.

It was right up this hill. She could see the guard rail.

So close, almost there.

The precipice was *right there*.

A snap sliced at the back of her ankle. The cold strike of teeth grazed her skin. Electricity bolted up her spine. Snarling howls violently raged behind her, its spittle stinging the back of her leg.

Faster. *Faster.*

She wasn't fast enough. She wouldn't make it. She would have to jump over the rail, but she had no energy left.

Almost there.

Her lungs heaved, and her legs burned. Another snarl sounded, but it seemed more distant. They were hanging back?

Didn't matter. It gave her a half second to catch her breath, drag stinging air into her overtaxed lungs.

She leaped over the guardrail and staggered forward.

Then she froze in place.

The dogs would be on her at any moment.

But she could not move.

Her brain refused to process the view.

She had reached the top of the peak. The viewpoint. The sight she'd longed to see for three devastating days. She'd made it. She had *won.*

But the ocean was gone.

An endless blistering desert lay where crisp blue water should have lapped at the cliff side. The stench of baking salt and seaweed burned her nose. Her lungs constricted from a single heaving gulp of the acrid air.

Her babies weren't here.

They hadn't made it.

There were no people. No survivors. No base camp. No help.

No hope.

Her knees threatened to collapse under her. The need to cry without tears made her eyes blister like acid. She wanted to scream but had no more voice. She wanted to pull out her hair but was too weak to lift her arms. She could wake up from this nightmare, but she wasn't sleeping.

She was alive. She *wanted* to live.

Earth wanted her dead.

A snapping growl jarred her out of her stupor and she whirled around, backing away from the dogs as they advanced.

Her foot hit the precipice and skidded in the sand.

Slipped off.

Her stomach dropped and her weight plunged backward.

And she fell over the edge of the cliff.

TWO

GOVEK

Govek stormed into his home, teeth gnashing, blood racing. The door frame cracked, splintering against the force he used to wrench it open.

His father, the mighty Chief Ergoth of Rove Wood Clan, wanted him gone, so Govek would get to it. He was leaving tonight. Right now. He refused to wallow in the muck at the outskirts of Rove Wood, begging for scraps for one moment longer.

Govek's rage was like a vise, gripping his chest with deadly strength, threatening to undo him. The anger bubbled up in his throat, burned at his tongue, and scorched his mind. It flooded him with the need to vent his fury. He would render his home to bits, tear the still living tree it was built within down in one mighty blow. Let the thundering boom of its trunk swallow up the vicious sounds of his clan eating merrily in the Hall while he was sent to his death.

His father was too grief-stricken to see reason, but his

brethren could have said something. They could have spoken on his behalf.

No one had.

Govek slashed at one wall, gouging his claws deep into the carved surface, destroying hours of work in a single strike. Hours of *his* work. Sitting here alone, with only the pops of his fire to break the ill-Faded silence. Painstakingly working vine and leaf patterns into his walls in a desperate attempt to drown out his loneliness.

He stayed away for them. To protect this clan from what he was—an abomination of the Fades, born with the same gifts to conjure magic that all his brethren in Rove Wood shared, but also with a vile disposition that tainted those gifts. Warrior strength that made that power too unpredictable. Too brutal. Too monstrous.

Even for the likes of orcs.

Govek raked his hand through his short, cropped hair. His palms were stinging. He'd made deep cuts from balling his fists to hide his wretched claws. Claws that refused to sheath even now. They'd never obeyed him.

He gulped in air. Forcing his blood to cool. He needed to *think*. But his rage had always held him in a tight grip. It had a life of its own, burning and prickling, as harsh as the cuts his claws had made.

He needed to pack.

Glancing about his small home, Govek felt a sharp pang of regret in his chest. He touched the place where he had ruined the design on his wall, glad that his outburst hadn't gone too far.

This dwelling his father had assigned so many years past had become both prison and refuge. Destroying it would only prove he was the threat his brethren believed him to be.

Finally, he saw sense. Rolling his shoulders back, he stomped into his bedroom, where he yanked his pack out from beneath the bed. Govek had made the leather pack himself, painstakingly working the hide of a great boar he'd slain in his bid for adulthood. It was still sturdy—after a full decade of prolonged use.

He'd never packed it to the brim as he intended to now, never prepared it for a lengthy journey.

He should have left Rove Wood a long time ago, joined his cousin Karthoc when he'd invited him into his forge so many seasons past. But instead, he'd stayed because only Rove Wood could harbor conjurers—wielders of Fade magic. The gifts blessed to the orcs born under their Great Rove Tree.

Gifts he, with his violent strength and uncontrolled temper, should never have had. He should be like his brethren—peaceful, quiet, and serene—instead, he was a monster. Built like a warrior, with bulging muscles and a blood-lust that simmered under his skin and made the magic he was born with deadly and chaotic.

Tavggol's words coursed through his mind, cooling his fury. *"You're a conjurer just like the rest of us, Govek. You belong here. The others will see that before long."*

Govek placed a hot hand over his burning eyes and took deep breaths into his lungs.

One full season had passed. Three miserable moons. Ninety-seven days.

Since they had killed his elder brother.

There was no reason for Govek to stay a moment longer.

He searched his trunk once more for extra clothing and discovered the cloak tucked away at the bottom. It was made from the same boar he'd proudly slain to make his pack. He'd worked tirelessly on it in his youth, when he'd been more foolish and prone to hope.

It was small in his hands and fitted for a female. A mate. He'd lined it with fox fur for warmth and treated the hide to be resistant to rainfall. It was in perfect condition, never worn. Not even by Yerina.

She would have scorned it, anyway. Demanded something prettier, something more delicate.

Govek scrubbed his hand over his face to push the thoughts of his former woman out of his mind. He turned his attention back to the cloak.

Perhaps he was still a fool because instead of tossing it away, he folded it and tucked it into his pack. It took up precious space that could have been used for other things, like extra clothes or tinctures.

Govek would carry his hope with him, though he held no illusion it may ever become reality.

He had only just settled it away when he heard someone walking up the darkened path. The slight creak of his bottom porch step alerted him, too quiet to be an orc, followed by the strong scent of sage wafting in.

Viravia.

He hefted his pack while bringing his lower jaw up to conceal his tusks and fangs. His jaw twinged with that familiar dull ache. The pain of contorting his face was almost like an old friend, allowing him to be in the presence of the few precious human females that made Rove Wood Clan their home without frightening them half to death. All his brethren performed this act, but with their much smaller teeth, it did not contort their features or cause them pain as it did him.

It couldn't be helped. He had long resigned himself to it. He was loath to make anyone any more fearful of him than they already were.

Especially his late brother's mate.

He came out of the bedroom and found Viravia still on his stoop. Her bright blue eyes were wide with shock after seeing his door half off its hinges. Proof that his fury was just as unhinged.

It was dangerous for her to be here, but she did it anyway. Tavggol's mate had always been brave.

And far too kind.

Govek moved toward her, and she scampered down to the bottom step. He resisted the urge to growl in frustration at her blatant fear. It cut him deep that his brother's widow would think he might harm her, even though he knew she had good reason to be wary.

"Control yourself, Govek. You are frightening the women," his father would remind him.

Govek clenched his fists. He could feel his blood thrumming through the corded veins of his neck because of the effort. Working to follow his father's advice, even though he despised it.

Why was he *never* in control? For the others, it came so easy.

If he hadn't been born with magic, he would never have had to worry about it. He could have vented his vile anger like all the other warrior orcs instead of hiding here in Rove Wood.

He would change that now. Magic or not, he would go.

Viravia's cheeks heated to a bright pink, and she tucked

her black hair behind her ear. Embarrassment was a very human emotion and Govek's irritation dimmed at the sight of it.

"Can I come in?" Her voice was a bare whisper.

He moved aside, backing away into his kitchen so she could enter without having to skirt around him. For what it was worth, she'd recovered from her fear before she crossed the threshold.

She was flush, chest rising and falling in soft tandem. Her cheeks still colored, lips red, and her hair was wind stroked. His late brother's mate was the epitome of human beauty.

It rendered Govek even more disgusted that he could think of his brother's woman this way.

He truly was vile.

He returned to the task of packing supplies from a cabinet he'd carved and oiled himself. The kitchen had been his own design, and he had used it far more often than an orc typically would. His hearth was lined with the stonework he'd chiseled. His furniture and trappings were all handwrought.

Perhaps another clan member would take it. One who would have no use for the full kitchen since they would be welcome to eat in the Hall. One who would put all four chairs at the table to use, visiting and playing betting games. Or enjoy the small seating area off the kitchen to its fullest, since they would spend their time in the company of others.

"You're . . . you're really going?"

He shot a glance at Viravia, his eyes lingering on her swollen stomach. She stroked her hand down it protectively, as any expectant mother would. "Yes."

Her breath left her in a rush. "Govek, you *can't*."

He snorted. His father thought otherwise. "I was given a command."

"A stupid, foolhardy command," Viravia said, earning a degree of interest from him. Most would not dare insult Chief Ergoth so plainly. She continued without preamble, ruining the wry humor Govek had gained. "You should take me on as your conquest, Govek."

Bubbling fury coated his throat and threatened to spill from his mouth. He kept his teeth clenched hard as he rasped, "No."

The woman's shoulders slumped. "I don't mean for us to be *mates*, Govek. Just partners, friends, and this babe is . . . he's already your kin. None would argue if you took him on as your son."

"No, Viravia," he managed, trying to keep the snarl from his tone.

"Tavggol would—"

Govek slammed his fist so hard into the wooden countertop it exploded, snapping off the corner. Viravia yipped and skittered away. His hand stung from the impact. The cuts on his palm broke open anew.

"Do not speak of what my brother would have wanted," Govek snarled. Tavggol was the only male in this fucking clan that had ever given a shit about him. He could never betray his brother in such a vicious way.

The idea of taking his brother's widow for his own mate made bile rise in his throat. And he could not risk the health and safety of his nephew by acting as his father.

Govek's brutal strength combined with his magic was too dangerous to be around anything so fragile and precious.

To her credit, Viravia did not flee.

Remorse clouded Govek's fury as he examined the

damage he'd done to his counter. His mind raked over the steps it would take to repair it. He managed to sheath his claws.

"You needn't worry, Viravia. Your child will be the next clan leader, as all here desire."

"I don't care about that."

Govek took pause, brow furrowed.

"All I want is for this clan to be safe so that he can grow without fear. In peace." She rubbed her pregnant stomach tenderly again and Govek's shoulders sagged.

It was an ill-begotten, but lovely, wish. One he knew his brother had held dear as well.

"This clan will be safer without me in it."

Viravia straightened, meeting his eyes. "That's not *true*. All the orcs in Rove Wood have magic. You aren't any different from them."

Govek nearly laughed at such a blatant *lie*. "Aren't any different? Has pregnancy made you *blind*?"

Viravia's brows pinched with hurt and Govek regretted his harsh words but could not take them back. Nor did Viravia have any to counter them. They both could see that Govek was not built the same as the slender, regal Rove Wood orcs. He had three times the muscle of the burliest male here.

He was built like a warrior. Like Warlord Karthoc, who was, even now, training his males at Baelrok Forge. Preparing them for gruesome battle. His cousin was determined to fight back against the Waking Order's slaughter.

Govek would join them. He would keep Rove Wood secure from the outside. He did not understand why he still gave a shit, but his gut clenched with the urge to protect these Fade-blessed woods.

"My cousin will not allow this clan to fall." Govek turned to his kitchen so he could continue packing. He tucked the hardened bread into a cloth napkin. "It is too vital."

"How can the *War*lord protect this clan from war when he is at the center of it?" The venom in Viravia's tone brought back Govek's wry amusement.

"My cousin is powerful and wise."

"Karthoc is a war-hungry twat who will bring more death here than can be measured by graves alone," Viravia spat, forcing an amused snort from Govek. To think this tiny slip of a female could spout such brave nonsense. He would have liked to see her face up to Karthoc.

Viravia hoped for peace, but peace between humans and orcs was all but doomed with war continuing to rage between them.

"If . . . if you won't take me, then I'll go to the Headman at Oakwall Village and speak for you."

Govek stilled.

"Your father can't possibly be sure that *every* woman there would spurn you. Not everyone believes what Yerina says. If you just told your side—"

"It doesn't matter." Govek's voice was so low it rumbled in his gut.

"But if I just—"

"No, Viravia." He refused to speak with her about this. With anyone. The clan could gossip, and the village could lob accusations, but in the end, what had happened between him and Yerina was private. Govek's truths were his own. There was no use trying to change anyone's mind. They wouldn't believe him, anyway. They didn't want to hear his excuses.

"You were never officially named the heir to the clan," Viravia said, her desperation rising in tandem with the tone of her voice. "And having a conquest in order to become the heir is a stupid tradition. Why, Savili told me not even your father honored it."

"This has never been about me finding a conquest, Viravia. No one actually wants me to sire a son," Govek said, meeting her eyes. "You know that as well as I."

This was about getting rid of him. Once and for all.

He balled his fists to hide his claws again.

"If you don't lead the clan, then who will?"

"Sythcol," Govek said, now remembering to pack healing tinctures. Magical ointments and salves that made Rove Wood Clan so important to the war efforts. It was the only reason his kind had not fallen to the Waking Order's plunder long ago.

"Sythcol and his conjurers are far too busy making tinctures for the orc warriors to find time to lead this clan," Viravia said.

"My father is in good health. He should be able to lead a long time. Long enough for your son to grow strong. And then he will lead this clan."

"You can't go to Estwill, Govek." Viravia's voice held a tremor. He clung to that tiny scrap of kindness like a drowning rat. "They'll *kill* you."

He said nothing to that obvious statement.

"Chief Ergoth must be wrong about the missives your mother sent from Estwill. There's no way she could have gotten them through, even with a messenger sparrow. And *five* women wanting to resettle here and become conquests to orcs? From a village overtaken by the Waking Order? It's madness."

It was. And so was sending your only living son to his death.

"Of course, I would know your mother's hand and scent above all others. Corine was my conquest, my mate, for six Fades-blessed years until you were born."

Ergoth's words blistered through his mind. Words spoken before the whole of the clan.

"Go and bring these women back. One will surely play conquest for you. And four other orcs will also be blessed with sons. The Fades smile upon us this day."

He barely withheld a growl as his rage spiked. Was his father delusional? Had Tavggol's death warped his mind?

Or did he despise Govek that much?

Govek gripped the tie of his pack and knotted it.

"You plan to martyr yourself, then." Her tone was hushed with reproach.

He had no intention of going anywhere near Estwill, but he had not the energy to explain his true plans to Viravia.

"You can't mean to leave right *now*," Viravia said as he moved past her and out the door.

Autumn swirled around him. The trees of Rove Wood were colored orange and red, flooding the land of Faeda with the last gasp of beauty before winter rendered their world dark and still.

Govek glanced toward the flickering firelight of his clan and breathed in the wood smoke and roasting meat.

Elk meat. His mind's eye flashed with the memory, seeing the prized elk he'd fought cooking over the fire in the Rove Wood Hall. Its flank slashed by deep gouges. Govek had worked so fucking hard to take down the elk quickly and painlessly while also ensuring not to damage it so every bit of the meat could be used, and then his father handed it over to a novice butcher who had ruined it.

"Govek, please," Viravia cried loudly. Her voice broke the stillness. She was trying to draw attention, but it was useless. There was no one around to hear, even if they could. Govek's dwelling was too far from any other clan member's home.

"Govek!" Viravia rushed forward, though she stopped short of touching him.

His eyes lingered on her rounded stomach. His thoughts turned to the future. "Goodbye, Viravia. I truly hope you and your son find the peace you crave."

With those parting words, Govek turned away and set out on his journey. He left his clan behind without a farewell and embraced whatever trials lay ahead of him, knowing at the depths of his soul that he would never return to Rove Wood Clan.

THE FIRST TWO days of travel were a blur. Govek knew these woods better than he knew himself. They were his most steadfast friend and greatest ally. They had kept him safe for all his seasons.

Then he reached the end of their safety.

The autumn had fallen hard on Rove Wood.

It was far too soon. It should have been at least another moon cycle, another thirty days, before the oaks and maples turned completely. The trees surrounding Govek were tinged with their brightest colors. Gold and red and orange, beautiful but unsettling.

The hunting had also become difficult. When Govek had first taken up the mantle of hunter for the clan, it had been easy to find large game. Now, ten summers later, the only thing left in abundance were the many fish in the Spring of the Fades.

The blight had reached Rove Woods despite its ancient history as the purest glen on the surface of Faeda.

But the Fades slept on, uncaring that the beings they created were in peril.

The Great Rove Tree, a relic of the Fades themselves, twined its roots with the other plant life. Extending its magic and protection for many leagues, but it could not touch all of Faeda.

Govek spent far too much time at that edge, staring down at the soil as if he might see the roots beneath. He was well aware of what it felt like to cross the magical barrier and was not looking forward to doing it again. Especially knowing these were his last moments in its sacred space. It was not like his journey with Karthoc, taken a full season ago, when Govek had known he would eventually return.

This was truly the last time.

The pull to return to Rove Wood, to go back to his clan, back to the Great Tree, was almost too much to endure. It sang in his veins, blistered up his spine, burrowed into every corner of his mind.

But he couldn't. He would not go back. And no amount of hesitation would make leaving easier.

Govek forced himself on, working past the prickling under his skin and the bone deep dread that flooded his mind, and crossed into the outer forest.

His senses felt stifled. Colors dimmed before his eyes. Red and yellow trees were muted. Evergreen bushes grayed.

The light too. It was as if midday had plunged into late afternoon. Even the chill in the air felt harsher.

The blurring numbness punctuated by the sharp pain of each heartbeat drove Govek to distraction.

When he was with Karthoc and his warriors on their journey to Clairton a season ago, he'd been able to ignore the pain by concentrating on the looming dread of Tavggol's disappearance. He'd focused on finding his brother. Rescuing him.

Govek balled his fists.

It had been warm then, midsummer heat baked the land. Now it was icy cold as winter steadily crept in.

The easy chatter of Karthoc's warriors had helped, too. Leaving Rove Wood made their heads turn foggy and muddled, as if the Fades themselves rebelled against orc kind leaving their blessed woods. For half a day, the warriors' ability to perceive threats, smell them on the air, hear them in the distance, had diminished, but with a group of twenty, it hardly mattered. They took care of each other.

Now, Govek was alone, and he could not help but turn irritable at the relentless throbbing in his muscles.

He knew he would grow accustomed to being outside the realm of the Rove Woods by nightfall, but until then, he would suffer.

He paused at a river. The roar of the current and glistening water beckoning him. Govek washed his face and neck in the icy current, considering the option of setting up camp for the rest of the day and letting the pain of leaving Rove Wood run its course. However, with naught but the flickering of firelight before him, Govek was certain his thoughts would turn dark.

A harsh squeal cut through his senses.

Govek whirled, claws instantly extended, and teeth bared. His eyes found the predator right off the bank.

A great boar. Slick brown fur, flat dripping nose, and beady black eyes. It was small for its kind, but still taller than he was by half a head. Its body was larger than that of three human horses. Its arched back and muscular body staggered toward him.

The boar was sick. Its thick hide was patchy, mouth foamed, and its eyes were clouded. It swayed as it took in Govek, as if drunk.

It had the blight.

The beast lunged toward him, and Govek dodged, storming into the river. Icy water raged around his legs. He wanted to cull the boar quickly, painlessly. It need not suffer any more than it already had. It squealed at him, charging. Govek leaped to the side. Its huge tusks nearly grazed him as it hurtled into deeper water. They were as long as his arm. They could stick him right through.

It lunged again, and Govek swung around, working to get to its jugular. He unhinged his jaw, gaping his maw. Cool air rushed into his throat as he readied to strike.

The animal slid on the slick rocks, its legs knocking and buckling. It went down.

Govek seized his opportunity and pounced. He raked his jaws into the boar's flesh, dragging his fangs across its neck, and speared deep to find its vein.

Thick blood spewed into his mouth, tasting of metal and rot. Govek jerked away and spat the blighted liquid into the river. He couldn't catch the blight from it, but it would make him sick to his stomach.

The animal squealed and its life slowly ebbed away. Its

death spasms dwindled. The water ran red, and Govek stepped away, watching, waiting for it to finally go still.

When it had, he rinsed his mouth out, washing the tainted blood away. Then went for a better look.

The tusks were altered—bound by spikes and sharpened to points.

His gut twisted. Humans. It had to be. None but humans of the Waking Order would stoop so low as to deform and bind one of the Fades great beasts to use for war.

But to use one that was clearly blighted? It seemed like folly. Judging from the boar's condition, it had been suffering from the curse for at least two seasons, but the rope looked fresh.

Perhaps the humans who had captured this boar were too dense to realize it had been tainted by blight?

Govek raked a hand through his hair, tugging at the short strands which brought clarity. Something wasn't right about this. Humans could be thickskulled, but using a boar like this was madness.

His hands came down to cut the leather straps away from the boar's tusks so it might journey to the Fades unaltered.

A disconcerting and very familiar scent wafted up. Something he knew but could not place. His mind was still too muddled from leaving Rove Wood. He leaned in for a better whiff and at the same moment the boar jerked up and skewered him with the spikes.

Right in his gut.

Govek roared, scrambling back, but it was too late. The current snagged him, caught his feet out from under his weight and dragged him into the water.

The rapids were quick and jagged with debris. He was

bashed into rocks and hurtled into logs. It took all his energy to keep his pack with him and hold his head above the water.

Damn the Fades for the part they played in this.

His elbow slammed into a stone, and pain ricocheted up his arm. The distraction was nearly his doom. A hidden boulder under the surface crushed his ribs and caused him to lose his breath. He went under, and his throat flooded with the crisp, icy water.

His pack floated, and he clung to it. It was the only thing that kept him alive.

Govek fought and pushed back the agony.

He choked on hard-won air.

A branch slashed his cheek, and he snatched it up. Water sprayed around his face and shoulder as he hung from the limb.

Thankfully, it held.

He clutched his lifeline and pulled his way to the bank. Bramble caught him at the edge, and rocks abraded his tattered flesh.

He lived. Fuck.

His chest heaved, so heavy it burned, and his vision blurred, but he found the strength to hoist himself up. He pushed through the blackberry patch using his pack as a shield. Every breath was agony, sharp and potent.

Sitting down to examine himself, he found his ribs were cracked.

Wrenching his pack open, Govek gripped one of his precious few tinctures, uncorked the vial's top and downed the bitter liquid in a single gulp. Heat bloomed through his body as the tincture healed him, slowly working its magic.

He was spent. Govek slumped to the muddy ground, taking a moment to catch his breath.

Barking broke the silence. The odor of wolves far too close skewered his senses.

A hunting pack had caught the scent of his blood.

The Fades truly wished him to suffer.

He was up on his feet, sprinting again, rushing through the woods. His legs throbbed and his chest exploded. His mind was in tatters.

Fuck the blight. Fuck the wolves. Fuck the Fades.

With his eyes trained to the sky, he was fathoming up more curses, when an unbelievable sight assaulted him.

A woman—a human woman—appeared out of thin air at the top of the tree line and fell.

Govek froze as she landed in a convenient pile of leaves. They billowed around her, cushioning the drop she'd sustained.

He reeled, confused and thunderstruck. What great magic had conjured her?

And then he was smacked with a devastatingly familiar sensation. It sparked in his veins, danced along his limbs, and clenched around his heart.

He shook his head to clear it and raked hands through his hair.

He must be mistaken. Imprinting did *not* work like this. It wasn't possible.

But the instinctual hum in his chest couldn't be denied.

The wolves bellowed too close. Just off the tree line.

He did not have time to think.

Fades help him.

THREE

MIRANDA

When Miranda was little and living in the group home, there was an enormous oak tree in the backyard. Every fall Mrs. Clark would give all the kids a rake and they would get the leaves into a massive pile. The bigger kids would take the younger children by their arms and legs and swing them into the pile. They would fall, laughing and screaming, into the damp foliage. The cool crunch engulfed them completely as the leaves fell over their noses and blocked out the sky.

Miranda still remembered the smell of it, crisp and clean. The taste too, as one or two leaves had been sucked into her mouth when she gasped from the exhilaration of the fall. She remembered looking up through the pile, seeing little pricks of blue sky through the gold leaves. It was a happy time. The best.

So, when she experienced that exact memory, she was certain she was dead. She lay on her back, looking up into the bright blue sky with gold and red leaves surrounding her, feeling weightless. She waited for pain, numbness, even the great booming voice of her maker. But she felt none of that. The sweet scent slowly filtered through the dirt and grime caked in her nose and mouth.

She sat up slowly, breaking through the leaves.

The canopy of autumn-glazed trees above her swayed in a gentle, but icy cold breeze. The smell of deep woods— pine and damp—had her gasping, heaving air into her lungs. Filling them up with life.

She pinched her thigh hard enough to bruise and felt pain. She waved her arms and the leaves she had fallen into rustled. In the distance, she heard the babbling of a brook. The sound made her parched mouth tingle with want.

Miranda looked around, unable to believe her own eyes, unable to understand where she was or what she was doing here.

There was no cliff. No dried-up ocean. No blistering sun or dead air.

She was in the center of a lush, beautiful forest. She dug her fingers into the leaves and ripped them up in her hands.

Miranda was not dead. She was not broken and bloody. Her life had not ended with a violent, crushing splat.

She had fallen, but something had caught her.

Something she knew in the depths of her soul did not belong to Earth.

Miranda examined one of the leaves with equal parts awe and confusion. She was no botanist, but she couldn't place ever seeing or hearing of a leaf that tapered off into spirals. The leaves above her were flooded with the circular patterns and dazzled with bright colors. Reds and yellows blended into a sight so glorious it stole her breath.

Her imagination must have been laboring in overdrive to conjure all this up.

She fell, right? She flexed her muscles, ran her hands over her goosebump-covered arms, torso, legs . . . nothing. She didn't feel any pain. No injuries at all.

So, this was a dream. The last gasp before her existence winked out. Any moment now, she'd see a bright light in a tunnel and know this was the end.

She sat tense, twirling the leaf. Her tattered running shorts were getting soaked through from the damp pile. Her tank top and sports bra did nothing to protect her from the frigid air.

Birds twittered, and Miranda stilled, jerking her gaze to the sky.

Birds. Flying right above her.

The trees rustled in a breeze.

This forest was so pretty. Dark trunks breaking into curling limbs that stretched toward the sky. Bright vibrant colors more dazzling than a fiery sunset coated them like a warm cloak. They rustled in a crisp gentle breeze, leaves breaking free and raining down to land upon rich green moss. It was unlike anything she'd ever seen on Earth.

This couldn't be real.

Miranda's throat worked, swallowing hard as she prepared for the delusion to end, waiting for this fantasy world to crumble. If she were lucky, the apocalyptic nightmare would disintegrate with it.

Or maybe she was having a complete psychotic breakdown. She'd listen to the delightful forest sounds and follow the singing birds back to a padded white room.

She inhaled. Deep wooded bliss filtered through the

muck of her sinuses. She was shaking hard enough that she dropped the mystery leaf into her lap.

She couldn't be alive. This wasn't real.

The sound of howling catapulted her into action.

The dogs had followed her. They'd chased her off the cliff. Those damn, horrible beasts that hunted her at every turn. She clawed at her bag, pulling it off her shoulder. She found it miraculous that the wind hadn't ripped it from her in the fall.

Miranda was about to bury herself in the leaf pile when she heard the stomping of feet, and she froze. Her heart skipped and breath caught.

Someone burst into the clearing.

Or rather *something*. Any sliver of doubt this wasn't an illusion conjured by her shattered mind was destroyed as she examined the inhuman male approaching her.

He was massive. Had at least half a foot on the tallest man she'd ever seen. He was easily seven feet. His shirt was torn open, revealing a chest rippled with muscles. His arms bulged under the tight sleeves of his shirt.

And they were green. His skin was *green.*

It wasn't a mild green either. Not the kind of green she could pass off as nausea or really bad concealer. He was *bright* green—new spring growth green. Hand him a jug and he could be the mascot for a limeade commercial.

Miranda was fairly certain By-Pass nuclear bombs didn't turn people green. They were more likely to melt your flesh clean off. Then again, her own skin wasn't melting, and she'd been at the epicenter.

The man was coming right at her, and the horrid dogs were still barking, getting closer. He reached out to grab her, to pull her up, but Miranda knew those monsters, and she was in no state to outrun them. Neither was this mystery guy. He had a distinct limp. He'd get picked off and eaten before you could say salsa verde.

She grabbed him first, by the wrist, wrenching him forward and caught him off balance. His eyes widened in shock, but he didn't fight the plummet into the leaves. With deft, practiced motions, Miranda pulled her bleach citrus spray out of her bag and spritzed a healthy layer over them before yanking the foliage up to cover them.

She hoped this green guy wasn't stupid enough to move or breathe while they were hiding, but she had no time to tell him to shush. The dogs broke through the tree line less than a second after she'd gone still. Their growls and snarls had her fighting the urge to tremble. They were so close. Any rustle of leaves would give away their hiding spot.

The sniffing continued, and Miranda found the courage to open her eyes, hoping by some miracle she could see what was going on through a gap between the leaves.

Instead, she came face-to-face with the mystery man, less than six inches from her.

She skittered her gaze down to the slope of his slightly crooked nose, to the jutting under-bite that made his face look squat and disproportionate, and to the wide span of his lips, which were a shade darker than the rest of his pea soup skin.

Wait, were those fangs?

No. Not fangs. The two sharp white points of his teeth jutted from his lower jaw so that made them tusks, right? They poked into his cheeks, and she resisted the urge to touch them, ensure they were actually there and not part of this radiation-induced delusion.

A low rumble sounded from him. Quiet enough that she

was certain she was the only one that could hear it or rather *felt* it. A deep, buttery vibration that turned her guts to mush and made her want to collapse into the fold of his embrace.

Dang, she was really being stupid now. The truth was, she'd been so starved for human contact it didn't matter where it came from. She would take a literal alien and be glad.

Was that what he was? An alien? She was certain the growing national tension had caused the apocalypse. World War V had been rolling on for ten years. It was a constant looming threat, smothering everyone like a blanket in sweltering summer heat.

She shifted her weight slightly and the leaves felt like prickly ice against her skin. She had to force herself not to shiver. The alien was still watching her. His harsh gaze was the only thing that kept her still.

Wouldn't it be her luck to have a fricking alien come down and abduct her in the final hour? Fly her off in a saucer bound for a laboratory. Get herself a nice vivisection before the radiation could melt the skin off her bones. She wasn't sure which fate would be worse, honestly.

Maybe she should alert the dogs and get herself eaten after all.

"Shh."

The hushing sound jerked her attention back to the man's eyes—emerald with flecks of gold.

Beautiful.

Was she dreaming or dead? Her throat constricted. She had plans, dang it! She wanted to move into an apartment she didn't hate. Get promoted at the bank. Apply to be a foster parent.

Leaves rustled next to her head, and she flinched. There

was a dog there. Right freaking there, holy shit, she really was going to get ripped apart.

It backed away, snorting. Its tail smacked a leaf or two and a tiny crack allowed her a good look at the creatures that had haunted her for days.

But it wasn't them.

The dogs from Earth were black and half rotting, with piercing eyes and foaming teeth.

These dogs were wolves. Gray. Clean. Healthy. Thick, glossy fur. Not a limp in sight.

Wolves had been wiped out a hundred years ago, hunted to extinction like most of the predatory animals. She'd only seen videos of them in ancient documentaries.

Miranda's eyes burned. What an amazing delusion!

"Shh," the alien shushed her again. This time, she felt a light brush on her hand. The stroke of his warm skin as he tapped her palm with firm fingers. The sensation of being touched after thinking she would never see another living being again rocked her right out of her already fraying senses.

She concentrated on his face, almost too scared to blink. She'd open her eyes to find herself alone and terrified all over again. Abandoned in the wasteland. Left to walk until...

She didn't want to die.

He tapped her harder, and she became painfully aware of how close the snarling and sniffing had become. As if they were already found.

She had lied. She wanted to be abducted, not ripped apart by wolves. Miranda gripped the alien's hand, clutching three of his thick fingers and prayed to any deity that might be around to hear her.

A distant howl sounded, low and sweet.

The clacking of the wolves running into the forest relaxed her chest. Both she and the green man froze in their places, listening for any sign that the animals might come back.

Then he burst up so quick that Miranda yelped, shocked at his intense speed. She'd hardly caught her breath when he grabbed her by the arm and yanked her out of the leaf pile. Debris rained down around them like they were in a tornado. The scent of decaying leaves flooded her nostrils, crisp and stark against her blistered sinuses.

Was this real? Could she dare to hope?

The tight grip on both her wrists caught her attention. The man dragged her forward, stilling her with the intensity of his gaze. She couldn't break away, even as he pulled a length of rope from his dark leather pack.

"Whatever plot you were scheming has failed, woman."

Her heart threatened to burst from her chest. He spoke. He could speak. She wanted to force him to say something else.

"Who are you?" He drew closer until she could feel the heat from his chest. He was so wonderfully *warm.* "What magic rendered you to these woods?"

"I . . . I don't . . ." Miranda's gaze skittered upward to the sky. "I fell off a cliff."

"*What*?" The alien rasped.

"I fell . . . fell and . . ."

She took a deep breath. This was a dream. Just a dream. She looked down at her hands, still held tight in the stranger's grip. His green skin was so stark against her peachy complexion. "I don't want to be tied up."

A fierce scowl crossed the man's features, deepening his

brow, darkening his eyes. Miranda's lips parted half from fear and half from some other stupid, irrational emotion that made her gut quiver and her blood tingle with heat.

"You are in no position to make demands of me, woman," he snapped before adjusting his grip so he could uncoil the rope.

She took advantage of his loosened hold and squiggled her hand free. He jerked to grab her again, but froze when, instead of bolting, Miranda reached up to touch his creased forehead.

His skin was cool and damp, like he'd just gotten out of a swimming pool. She soothed the lines away, stroking until he finally relaxed.

Dang, his eyes were so pretty. Green and gold with long lashes. She'd really worked up someone right out of her own fantasies, well, except for maybe the green part. And why freaking not? Might as well spend her last few minutes in bliss.

The male sucked in a harsh breath, distracting her from her lusty thoughts. And then he dipped down. Electric spikes zapped her spine as he buried his nose in her neck and inhaled deeply.

Oh goddamn! Was this shifting into a *wet* dream? She wouldn't argue if it was.

He exhaled harsh against her skin. Snorting. Coughing. He jerked away and rubbed at his face, dropping her hands.

"Are you okay?" she asked, her stomach knotting at the knowledge that she probably smelled like absolute shit. Bleach and sweat and fallout grime. "I'm sorry. I haven't had a bath in way too long. I promise, I don't smell this bad on a usual day. I've got like, vanilla body lotion and this really nice, sweet pea scented hand cream." She broke off, tongue too parched to babble on. Not that her hygiene routine was of any flipping interest to this alien.

But after looking at his wide, attentive eyes, she realized maybe it was? He was watching her so intently it made her skin prickle. Then he raked a massive hand over his face and shuddered out a harsh breath.

He bridged the gap between them again, chest so close to hers she could feel the heat of his skin. The warm pine scent of him drew her in, made her squirm.

He gripped her wrists.

"You are now my . . . conquest." His voice was so low it tingled up her spine and warmed her gut.

"What?" She didn't care what he was saying as long as he kept at it.

"No other humans would dare venture into the depths of these woods, so do not hold folly that you may be rescued." His vibrant emerald eyes focused on her hands.

"But aren't *you* rescuing me?"

He froze.

"Don't tie me up," she said firmly. This was a dream, so she could control it.

He held the rope over her hands, hesitant.

She waited for him to obey. And he did.

He let her go and swung a heavy leather pack down to his feet, putting the rope away within its depths. The thing was soaking wet, just like the rest of him.

"If you try to flee. I will catch you and bind you."

"Okay. So, I'll only run when I'm ready to be tied up," she mumbled before she could think better of it.

The male's eyes snapped to her again, flickered over her body for half a second. He shuddered, raked a hand through his hair, and muttered something she couldn't make out before replying at a normal volume. "You . . . will tell me how you got here. Now."

Her throat closed. "I told you. I fell off a cliff."

"There are no *cliffs* here, woman."

"Yeah, that's pretty crazy, huh? This whole place is crazy." Miranda looked around again. "It's amazing how much the brain can conjure up just from watching kids' movies on repeat."

"You have children?"

"Uh, no. I mean, none of my own." Her eyes prickled but she was too dehydrated to produce any tears. Her heart pounded, and her ears rang.

Oh, god! She'd been trying not to think about it, and suddenly, all the little faces she'd taken care of at the daycare were reeling in front of her mind's eye and she couldn't escape.

She should have been there with them when the bomb dropped.

She belonged with *them*, not here.

She should have died with them.

A gust of wind ripped across her back, flinging her hair in front of her face. She shuddered in the icy chill. Dang, this place was *cold*. Nothing on Earth had ever been this cold.

"I don't . . . belong here," she whispered.

"You belong with me."

The crisp retort was so outrageous she huffed, opening her eyes to find the alien's green coloring had lightened up. His eyes had gone wide. Apparently, his declaration had shocked him, too.

But she had no desire to fight him on it.

She had lost her mind, and she was too tired, too

defeated, to care. Despite that, she found the wherewithal to ask, "Are you going to hurt me?"

His fierce eyes leveled her again, assessing. "That is the last thing I wish, human."

So, he knew what species she was. She couldn't guess his. He clearly wasn't human, though he had the general shape of one. Two arms and two legs. Symmetrical face. Hair that was cut jaggedly and fell in wet clumps across his brow.

She reached up and brushed those strands away. The male stilled, blinking, and when she removed her hand, he recovered.

"Should you have need or pain, you will state it, and I will provide remedy."

His words were odd, but the intention was clear enough. "I'm thirsty."

His brows rose in surprise, as if he hadn't thought she would actually ask him for something.

He reached into his pack, produced a soft leather pouch, and uncorked it.

What was this, the Middle Ages?

He handed it to her, and she struggled to get it into a suitable position. She almost dropped it, startling the man into gripping it. His hand covered the entire lower half of the bag while both her hands could only manage the top quarter.

"What are you?" she finally asked. Her gaze was stuck on his huge hands.

He jumped. His green eyes grew wide and dark brows rose. The expression of pure, unabashed confusion was adorable. "What?"

"What are you? Or are you a human in some kind of cosplay?"

"Cos . . .? I am an orc."

That's when Miranda knew for certain she was in a delusion of her own making. "An orc? Like from a fantasy novel?" His brows pinched together, and she wanted to smooth it again, but her hands were full. "You don't look like an orc. Aren't orcs supposed to be ugly? Like rotting flesh and crooked teeth?"

Once again, he was flummoxed. His jaw was even a little slacked, which let her see his lower tusks better. His under-bite was extreme, hiding his upper lip beneath it.

Then anger contorted his features. His jaw lowered more, making his face less squat.

He looked good. Scary, but good. She'd have to figure out how to irritate him more often.

"You humans may have dwindled our numbers, but I still find it unbelievable that you have never seen an orc before today. Regardless, you will come with me. And if you try to flee, I *will* hunt you. Do you understand?"

"Pretty much." She was in no condition to run away from him, even if she wanted to. Finally, she lifted the pouch to her lips.

She expected straight sand to pour into her mouth. She had no faith in her own imagination anymore.

But she got water.

Clean, crisp, cool water. It drenched her tongue, flooded her throat. Her gulps turned frantic as she sucked down as much as she could.

"Stop. Woman, stop!"

The orc tore the bag away from her, and she let out a

pitiful whimper. The man's face contorted again with an emotion she couldn't read.

"Woman, you will make yourself ill."

"Miranda."

"What?"

"My name is Miranda. You should know that as a figment of my imagination."

He paused, looking her over. "I am not an imagining, woman."

"Sure. Can I have the water back?" She would have tackled him for it if she wasn't so worried about him dropping the precious thing and spilling it. Her mouth had just started to taste like something other than mud when he'd ripped it away.

"Slowly," he demanded, pressing the nozzle to her lips again. He gripped the bag, stopping her when she tried to pull it closer. Drink faster. She could only manage a few sips at a time.

He was cruel. She couldn't get sick in her own dream. Or she supposed she could, but it wouldn't matter. She was about to throw a fit over it when he took it away and reached back into his bag, producing something that looked like bread.

The water was forgotten as he held the delectable roll in front of her face. "I will give you this, if you follow willingly and do not try to flee."

"I would literally follow you right off another cliff for that."

He continued to look puzzled, but handed over the bread. Snatching it, she shoved half of it into her mouth.

"Eat slowly," he demanded. "Or I will reach in and take it back."

Was he going to reach down her throat and into her stomach? She decided not to test the physics of this dream and obeyed the order. The bread was too hard to eat quickly, anyway.

He let her finish two rolls and have another long drink before closing up shop. Her abdomen felt like it was bulging against her shirt, but her brain was demanding she tackle him to the ground and steal every crumb of food and drop of liquid he had.

She distracted herself from attacking him as he produced a thick cloak out of his pack. It was so bulky she wasn't sure how he'd managed to fit it in there.

With both hands he held it up, his face questioning. Miranda blinked. "Is that for me?"

"If you are willing."

"Heck yeah, I'm willing." Her clothes were in tatters and this delusion was cold. Half the leaves were off the trees and the sun was low in the sky. She stepped forward, taking advantage of his shock, and swiped it out of his grip, only to fumble with the knot that closed the top.

"Would you like help?" He was laughing at her, she could tell.

"Yeah."

He made such quick work of the knot, which forced her to blush. Apparently, she'd lost her finger dexterity along with her mind.

The stranger stepped forward, slinging the cloak around her shoulders. He was so close she could feel heat radiating off him. He smelled of wood smoke and . . . blood.

"Are you hurt?" she asked as he secured the tie at her neck.

"No."

The abrupt way he denied it betrayed him, but if he wanted to play the tough guy, she didn't care.

Using what little stamina she had left, Miranda convinced herself that everything would be fine, that her mind wasn't stuck in a delusion while her body was bleeding out at the bottom of a cliff. Maybe even that Earth hadn't been destroyed and she would wake up in her bed at any moment.

"You belong to me, woman," the orc said, shouldering his pack. "Now come, it is time to leave."

CHAPTER

FOUR

GOVEK

G ovek was in agony.

The boar had gouged out a chunk of his side. One healing tincture hadn't been enough, but he was loath to use another, especially since the Spring of the Fades was close enough to spit in.

His senses were still fucking muddled from leaving Rove Wood, and now his nose was scorched, blistered, and aching. Whatever vile tincture the woman—Miranda—had used to throw off the wolves had burned him as well.

Fuck his raging instincts back to the Fades who'd given them to him. If he hadn't been so desperate to get a taste of the woman's true scent, he wouldn't be half gone right now.

Why did his base urges always lure him right toward the women he should avoid?

"Do I belong *to* you or *with* you?"

Govek sucked in a shuddering breath as the woman's

voice tingled through him like a balm. He should not have scented her. Should not have given into his wretched urges, but the damage was done. Fucking *done*.

She was imprinting within him. Her essence was soaking into his mind and connecting her to his being. He could feel her presence like a gentle hum in his head, steady and unyielding.

"Did you hear me?" Her warm fingers brushed the back of his wrist and Govek was crushed by the longing to wrench her off her feet and into his arms.

Why did she keep touching him? Didn't she see what he was?

"Before you said I belonged '*with*' you, and now you say I belong '*to*' you."

He did not think there was much of a difference. This woman's speech was so strange. Her every move and word clouded his mind.

He'd seen her fall out of the fucking sky like a Fades-blasted conjuring.

"Are you of the Waking Order?" Govek snarled, too low, too viciously. He'd terrify her, and she'd flee, and his instincts would force him to give chase. Such exertion would cause his puncture to worsen, and it would be sheer torture trying to hunt her down.

He should have bound her. Then she wouldn't be able to run. The beastly desire had his fingers itching to retrieve the rope from his pack.

"You mentioned that already. Is it some sort of club?" She sidled up close enough that he could feel her warmth radiating against his tender flesh. She looked so fucking good in the cloak he'd made. He wished he could scent her again, but if he got too close, her tincture would wound him further.

But under it, on those few patches of skin not doused in the vile concoction, she smelled better than any female he had ever been near. Like honey and crisp morning sun.

Fuck! What was wrong with him? He should try to stop the imprint, not strengthen it.

She continued to chatter. "I'm not a member of any clubs. I don't have time for them. I work two full-time jobs just to afford my apartment. Three, if you count the under-the-table babysitting gigs."

His brow twitched. She sat on babies?

"Gosh, the Youngs asked me to babysit next week, didn't they? They pay really good, but dang, it's a chore. I love Taylor, but she's a menace sometimes. Her tantrums are loud enough to piss off the next town over."

The woman trailed off and a haunting expression dimmed her features. Her eyes grew misty, and her voice trembled. "They're all dead."

His claws extended. "Dead?"

She snapped to attention, hugging herself tight. Whatever had happened to these babies she'd sat on was clearly weighing on her mind.

And her existence wore on his.

"How did you get here?" Something wasn't right with her. Humans didn't have magic. She shouldn't have been able to just *appear*.

Was she a trap? Why was she babbling about death?

Her haunted brown eyes pierced into his soul and hooked in his gut.

"I don't know. I was in my world, and then I got chased

off a cliff." She shook her head, looked off into the woods again. "I must be dreaming."

"In my world." She was from a different *world*?

He should leave her here in the woods.

That thought had his veins bursting with heat, scorching him from the inside out.

He was imprinting *hard*.

And that was fucking nonsense, too. It should have taken at least the full length of a moon before imprinting even *began*. Yerina's imprint hadn't set inside him until almost a full season had passed.

Yet somehow, this woman was thoroughly embedded after he'd simply watched her fall out of the air.

He'd heard of instant imprinting before, but in *legends* —stories told to children. He had never heard of a single occurrence where it had been real.

"It's so pretty," she said, more to herself than to him. "I can't believe my brain imagined all this. I hope I . . ." She stopped walking, her eyes skewered a golden coneflower, half withered in the mud at the base of a barren oak. "I hope I don't come to before I die."

His heart seized at the thought. "This isn't an imagining, and you will not die, woman. You are my conquest."

For the will of Fades! *Why* did he keep calling her that? She wasn't his blasted conquest. He wasn't going to *take* a conquest. He was going to war. To Baelrok Forge, where Karthoc's legions trained.

She finally glanced away from the flower. "Your conquest, huh? What exactly does that mean?"

She didn't know what a conquest was. Where the fuck was she *from*?

Govek ground his teeth. He should *leave her here*.

And then she reached out her blasted, warm, perfect fingers to touch his arm. It had been so Fades-wretched long since he'd been honored with such gentleness, and his mind was in blazing tatters.

And her imprint raged deeper.

"I will care for you," he finally managed. The truth of it stung his throat. He'd spent far too many miserable hours trying to care for his prior woman, only to have it all crumble around him. He'd given *everything* to Yerina. All that he had the power to give.

And it wasn't enough.

There was no overcoming his own vile nature and lack of control. He could only hide it for a short time before it finally bubbled to the surface.

"That sounds really nice," she whispered.

His heart thundered so hard it warmed up his chest. Miranda's eyes were so soft on him they may as well have been the rapids he'd just endured. She wrenched him under with her tenderness and he helplessly allowed her to batter him.

"Where are we going?" she asked before he regained his senses. "Or are we just going to wander about in the woods for a while? I'm fine with that, by the way. Wandering around. It's . . ." She fixated on a flock of robins flying overhead. Their arrow formation pointed toward the Rove Tree, and Govek clenched his fists.

It was too blasted early for them to be abandoning the outer woods for the protection the Great Tree offered. Winter was coming on hard.

"Tough guy? You okay?"

He scowled. "My name is Govek, woman."

"Call me Miranda, and maybe I'll call you by your name, too."

He growled low in his throat, the sound a threatening reverberation that sent the birds who had been chattering pleasantly into uneasy silence.

The female did nothing but raise her dainty brows in interest. She rubbed at her chest. An area he had been desperately trying to avoid staring at. "Ooh. That's tingly. How do you do that?"

He had never met a challenge quite the likes of this human, and his curiosity grew greater than his reservations. He took a moment to examine her fragile form. She was average height for a woman, which meant she only came up to the middle of his chest. She was wearing fucking *scraps*, and the cloak he'd given her wasn't tied together properly. Her waist was so slender he could span it with two hands. Her cheeks were ashen, the bags under her light brown eyes were heavy, and her hair was so matted and unwashed he could not discern what the actual color was.

She was not an impressive specimen to behold. Certainly not the kind of creature he would have thought could withstand his threats.

A caress to his forehead caused him to realize how close he had leaned into her.

Too close. The sweet, honeyed scent of her managed through his muddled senses and skewered his gut. It sent his mind spiraling into fractures and made his knees want to crumble.

Then her fucking tincture started to *burn*.

"You don't look so good." She stroked her fingertips along his forehead before covering it with her palm. "You're really hot. Er—I mean temperature wise, not attractive wise. Not that you aren't attractive because you totally are, I just—Dang it. Uh—" She backed away, cheeks bright pink.

Govek gulped, hardly able to keep up with her frantic babbling.

"Just . . . just forget I said anything," she said. "You have a fever. Or I think you do. I don't know what orc body temperature is supposed to be, but you weren't that hot a few minutes ago. Are you sick?"

Fever? He forced himself to straighten, reassess his condition.

He pressed back his soaked woolen cloak to take stock of the gouge.

"That . . . looks bad."

Distracted from the task, he glanced at Miranda's pale face, her trembling frame.

"That looks like . . ." Her wide eyes fixed on his side. "Looks like something you might get from falling off a cliff."

What was this insane babbling about? Why was she so Fades-wretched confusing? "I got this from a boar."

"A boar?" Her brow furrowed. "You mean like a pig?"

"Yes. One with spikes at the base of its great tusks." He took a threatening step nearer. "Did you have anything to do with that?"

It wasn't logical. He knew that the moment the words left his lips. Of course, she didn't have anything to do with the boar.

And yet he stalked nearer still, looming over her, his very bones wanting to render the truths out of her throat by force.

She fucking bridged the gap between them and lifted the

edge of his shirt so she could look at the injury again. Govek froze, shock icing him over.

Her hands were so blasted tender as they grazed his flesh. It made him forget the throbbing agony. "Oh, man, this looks really, *really* bad. Do you have bandages or anything? I can patch you up."

Govek adjusted to finally look at himself and his chest seized with shock.

Rapidly, he became aware of his physical condition. He'd been so caught up in the woman he hadn't realized how hard he was breathing or how clammy his skin was. Beads of sweat dripped from his forehead, and his left hip was going numb.

"Are you okay?" His conquest's worry cut through him. "Are you going into shock? Sit down."

Ignoring her order, Govek ripped the edge of his shirt away to get a better look at his puncture wound. He found it grisly—oozing blood and pus. Black veins snaked from the hole like shattered glass. His whole side was turning purple.

"Goblin poison. Fuck."

How the humans had gotten their hands on goblin poison was beyond him, but it did not bode well for the Under-Dwellers. Apparently, their retreat into the structure of Faeda had not been deep enough.

"What's goblin poison?" Miranda asked with not nearly the amount of worry one would usually have speaking those words. "What *are* goblins?"

He couldn't answer her. His mind was foggy and his limbs were starting to tingle with the telltale numbness that came before full paralysis hit.

Paralysis that led to inevitable death.

"Fuck," he raged, though it came out slurred and sounded odd.

He flung his pack off his shoulder, finding the task alarmingly difficult, and tried to open it. There was nothing inside that would help him. There were no orc-made tinctures strong enough to fight goblin magic.

The Spring of the Fades was his only hope. It would heal him. He turned toward it, only to have his legs collapse. He hit the ground hard, but barely felt it.

The woman said something that sounded like a question, but he was too busy getting his muscles to obey his commands to pay her any attention.

But he should have. He needed aid.

Aid from her? He didn't even know where she had come from.

His energy evaporated in waves and he laid down on his back in the wet leaves.

"What are you doing? I meant just *sit* down. Okay, fine. You do you," the woman conceded.

His eyes were blurry, but he could still make her out. "Fade Spring."

"What?" She settled down next to him. Her brow furrowed. "Let me help you back up." She tried to pull on him, groaning with exertion. He could sense the pressure of her grip on his arm, but couldn't feel the warmth.

"Spring," he gasped, pointing a single finger as she lifted his arm. She was so fucking weak. "Water. Drench out the . . . poison."

"A spring?" She looked into the woods. "Where? I don't see it."

For fuck's sake. He wasn't even surprised. Not a single person in this miserable world gave a fuck if he died here in the dirt. He shouldn't have expected this mystery woman to either.

For all he knew, *she* was the one who had poisoned him. Or at least was in league with the humans who had trussed up the boar. They'd stolen goblin poison. They could have stolen magic that could make her fall from the sky, too.

Though . . . for the life of him, he could not recall *any* being on Faeda ever having such powerful skills.

It didn't matter if he understood it or not. His life depended on her.

"H-hurry," he managed, closing his eyes. He wouldn't be able to blink in a moment and he didn't want to be trapped with them open. "Water."

He heard the wind in the trees, the fidgeting of the woman as she got a little closer. The frigid grip of numbness sliced over his senses. Filling out his chest. Pulling down his limbs. He could not even feel the air going into his nose and throat. The only way he knew he still breathed was by the simple fact that he hadn't passed out yet.

And he would soon.

Panic raged through him and it hardly registered because he was already so fucking *gone*. At least he could still hear.

"Huh. Well, this is suddenly boring."

Govek wished he couldn't hear after all.

Though, he supposed now would be the time she would bring out her cohorts, and he'd learn the truth of how she had gotten here. One mystery solved before he breathed his last.

"Should I continue on without you? But like . . . where?"

She didn't know where to go?

"I'mma get so lost if I go anywhere. I've never had good navigational skills to begin with. Though I guess since I don't really have a destination, I can't get lost. Hm, kinda tricky, that one. Can you get lost if you have nowhere to go?"

What was she rambling about now? Was no one coming to fetch her?

Was she . . . really alone?

As alone as he was?

"This is an awfully nice dream, but it's a little cold. And I'd rather be completely distracted."

Completely distracted from *what*?

"Dreaming about you just lying here isn't exciting enough. Maybe I should fathom up a carnival next?"

Oh, for *fuck's* sake.

This was it. He was going to die. He was going to suffocate next to a crazy woman who thought she was in a fucking dream.

Her dream. His nightmare.

"Hm, not working."

Was she honestly trying to create entertainment for herself?

"I'd rather you just wake up, though. You can get up now."

Sure, I'll get right on that.

"No seriously. Get up." There was another pause. "You're worse. Why are you getting worse? Why can't I control anything?"

He raged with the need to yell at her and yank her from her insanity.

If she hadn't come here to kill or capture him, then she should hurry up and *save* him.

"I really don't want to be alone."

If she didn't want to be alone, she needed to go get the *fucking water*.

"Get up now, please. Really. Up you get." She made a sound like she'd just tried to lift him, but he didn't feel it.

It was almost like floating in an abyss. Relaxing, if he could forget he was moments away from his demise.

"Okay, okay. This isn't working. I wonder . . ." Rustling sounded nearby. "Look, dude, I'm stealing your stuff. Wake up and stop me." She was digging through his pack.

Some of his panic ebbed to make way for amusement.

"Let's see, what else do we have—ow!"

Amusement over. His instincts roared to life, fighting hard against the poison. She was fucking injured. He could smell the blood, and he couldn't do a blasted thing about it.

"That hurt. I'm hurt. Dreams don't hurt."

The fear in her tone was agony.

"Dreams don't hurt. This . . . this is real. Is this real?"

He wished he could answer her.

"Please get up now."

Then the truth of it all hit her, and fuck, he almost wished she'd go back to blissful ignorance.

"Oh god, oh my god. Okay. Okay, you said . . . where's the water pouch?"

Govek would have held his breath if he had control of that.

"Okay, I'll be back. I'll be . . ." Her feet pounded on the hard ground, and her voice faded.

Govek almost never called to the Fades for aid. They had answered so rarely, but he was not above begging this time. Begging for her life as well as his.

It seemed like an eternity. Long enough he feared she hadn't made it. What if a predator picked her off?

Fuck! He'd never fought so hard in his life. He willed his muscles to move, and heaved his focus, but all that hit was a dizzying sensation suggesting his lungs were losing their ability to expand.

Then the snapping of a branch met his ears. He heard her heavy breath next. He'd never heard anything so blissful.

"Okay," she was breathless. Fabric rustled and ripped as she uncovered his wound. He heard splashing and knew she was pouring the water on him, but he still couldn't feel it. "Okay, was that enough? Is that working? Oh god! I don't know what I'm doing—help!"

No! She would bring every predator within twenty leagues.

"Help! Is anyone out there? Please! We need a doctor!"

A *doctor*? What is that? Did she mean healer? Her words were so strange. And her clothing was so odd and unfit for the cold weather. His nose could usually pick up individual ingredients within any stew or tincture he came across.

There wasn't a single plant or potion within *her* tincture that he could recognize.

Because . . . they were not from Faeda.

She'd fallen from the sky.

And no one was coming to her aid.

Any thought that she may have been laying a trap, that she might have been deceiving him, died away.

Was she truly from another *world*?

Blast, what were the Fades doing to him?

"I'll be back, I swear." He heard her rapid footfalls dying in the distance as she ran from him.

Panic roared through him. She'd just called every predator in the near vicinity and now she was tromping through the woods like the easiest of targets. Had she no sense at all?

If he'd thought the wait before was an eternity, this one was eons. It left him quaking in miserable madness. And even worse, he was getting his feeling back, but could barely twitch a finger.

He would be able to hear Miranda screaming in agony as she was torn apart, scent her blood in the air, but wouldn't be able to fucking move.

This fucking worthless imprint. Gifting him the ability to scent her on the wind. Hear her call him at great distances. The instinctual drive to cleave to her would thrum and burn while he listened to her be *eaten alive*.

"Okay!"

He hadn't even heard her run up, he'd been so caught in his panic.

"I got more." This time, when she dumped it on him, he felt a slight tingling. "I think . . . I think it's working."

It is. Stay the fuck here.

"I'll get more."

No!

She was gone, and Govek would be as insane as she was by the end of this.

He strained all his senses against the goblin poison, trying to feel her in the dark void of his mind. His blackened vision was prickling with dappled color as he tried to open his eyes.

Finally, she was back, drenching him again. He wished

she'd dump it on his head. Heal his burned nose so he could more easily scent for any predators around them.

She touched his side, and he felt the pressure.

"It worked. I can't believe that worked. That shouldn't have worked. It's flipping *water*." There was a shuffling sound, then ripping. "Bandages. Okay, I've got this. I've got first aid training. I know what I'm doing. If I can get Kenny Frits's bloody chin patched up, I can handle this, right? Right. I mean, he's not even wiggly like Kenny was. God, I wish you would wiggle. *Please* move."

More pressure against his side. He didn't need bandages. With the amount of spring water she'd dumped on him, he would likely be healed enough to get up soon.

"Why are you so freaking heavy," she grunted. He could feel her moving him this time, but only the pressure of it. There was no warmth or texture yet.

"There, there. More water."

Fades, please tell her he did not need *more* water.

They did not aid in this. As usual. She drenched him again. "Should I go get more?"

Frustration made his hands clench slightly. If his claws extended, she didn't notice.

"Please wake up. The black vein thing is gone now. Why won't you wake up?"

Warmth pressed into his torso. The tickle of hair.

She was resting *her head* on his *bare chest*?

Govek focused on that sensation. He had never in his life had someone rest on him this way. He wished he could feel it properly.

"Your heart sounds okay." Her hushed tone raked over him. "Dang, you smell good. What do you bathe in? Pine trees?"

He was uncertain how to process such a compliment.

"Okay. He'll wake up soon. It's okay."

He would. He could almost get his eyelids to twitch.

"Five things I can see. His healed wounds, his chest rising"—she paused as if looking around—"weird trees, red autumn leaves, and birds. So many birds. Four things I can touch."

What was she doing now? What was the point of this?

"His chest . . . again." Her hand stroked down his flesh. A *warm* hand. He would have groaned if he could have.

Her fingers trailed down his arm to his wrist, clasped it tight. "His heartbeat. My wet clothes and the cold ground. Three things I can hear. Heartbeat again. Birds too. Wind in the trees."

Govek noted that she sounded much calmer. Her breathing was deep, her voice was almost musical and slow. This was relaxing her. And him too.

"Two smells." She sucked in a lungful of air and breathed deep. "Man, you really smell good, and I smell like bleach."

Bleach. Was that the name of the tincture she was coated in?

Her lips fluttered over his heart. "One taste."

Govek sucked in a breath as his eyes popped open.

"Oh, my god, you're awake! Are you okay? Can you talk?"

He forced himself up on an elbow, only to nearly fall right back over. "Shirt."

"Shirt?" she repeated dumbly.

"Your fucking shirt," he grated out, each word hard won. "Where is it?"

She looked down as if she'd only just noticed she was only wearing a thin garment that barely covered her full, plump breasts. It held them tight to her body, pressed them up and together. He could easily see the outline of her nipples through the cloth. His fingers twitched with want to touch her.

The Fades really were testing him.

"Oh," Miranda covered herself with the cloak. The one he'd given her. It still looked fucking good on her, but not nearly as good as her naked torso. "I used it for . . ." She looked down at his wounds.

Following her eyeline, he saw she'd ripped up her shirt and wrapped it around the puncture wound. He tore the useless fabric off and revealed nothing but smooth, undamaged skin.

Miranda gasped and her hands pressed into his side, fingers splayed against his flesh. They were deliciously warm. "Oh, my gosh! That *really* worked. How did it do that? It's like magic or something."

"It *is* magic," he muttered. "Where are you hurt?"

She ignored his question. "Magic. Are you serious? You're not kidding. Oh my god. What is going on with this? How did I get here?"

Questions he also wanted the answers to, but there were far more pressing matters at hand. "I need to get to the spring."

"Oh," she exclaimed, scrambling to her feet. She tucked the cloak around herself in a way that concealed every part of her body he desperately wanted to get a better look at. "Let me help you."

His snort of a laugh came out more like a choked gulp. He'd crush her to a pulp under his weight. As if to prove it, she slipped her hand into his, gripping his wrist and trying to pull him up.

"I can help—"

He yanked away, careful not to touch her with his fingers—his fucking claws were threatening to extend—and laboriously he managed to get his feet underneath him.

"Okay. I guess you're really . . . you're all right?"

He was wavering slightly, but he would make it. "Just lead the way."

She stepped closer, completely undaunted, and took his arm. He was so startled by her actions he simply let her.

CHAPTER

FIVE

MIRANDA

Miranda held his arm tight as she guided him toward the spring, though she seemed to need his support more than he needed hers. Her legs felt like Jell-O. The adrenaline was wearing off and reality was setting in.

She couldn't start crying now. She needed to be able to see, but her eyes were burning with unshed tears, her throat was closed up, and her stomach was clenched tight.

Everything that had happened on Earth was real.

Her planet was gone.

Hollow dread opened in her chest and her lips began to tremble.

"Fuck! It was this close?" The orc cut in. His low voice helped soothe her somewhat. Like a purr, almost.

The trek really wasn't far. Just a hundred feet or so. Otherwise, she would never have found it. She would have gotten lost in her panic to heal him and wandered alone in the woods until she'd fallen from exhaustion.

He'd almost died because of her stupidity. "I'm so sorry."

He didn't respond other than to grunt.

Breaking through the trees, the sunlight spilled through the thinning canopy and illuminated the spring, giving Miranda her first good look at it. She hadn't taken the time when she was filling the water pouch.

It was breathtaking. Smooth stones lined the beach where perfect, clear water lapped at them. The pool was ovular, with a slim inlet off one side and no visible outlet. The current created gentle ripples in the water. The reflections of the brilliant red sunset sparkled against the rippling waves, making it appear to glow from within. Dark green moss and brightly colored leaves covered the surrounding surfaces. Each gust had more leaves raining down, like colorful snow. They landed in the water, swirling lazily—bright red and orange against crystal blue.

The sight was like nothing Miranda had ever experienced. Unearthly bliss. Pure perfection. She sucked in a breath of crisp evening air, the fragrance of clean soil and fresh water so poignant she could taste it.

"Stay here."

Miranda flinched as her companion tugged away. "R-right here? Where are you going? What if the wolves—"

He hummed darkly, though she couldn't tell if the sound was one of irritation or thought. He nodded toward a boulder. "I can lift you onto that."

The rock was taller than she was and covered in soft moss. "Okay."

The male hesitated, as if he hadn't expected her to agree. His hands were still balled into fists and Miranda was suddenly fighting the urge to stroke them into relaxing.

Then he stepped forward. His hands lingered on her hips, and he hoisted her upward. He plopped her down and quickly removed his hands. Her skin tingled at the loss. Miranda said nothing, just brought her knees up to hug them. The orc swung off his cloak and placed it over the top of her legs, wrapping her up in its warmth and rich pine scent. It was oddly dry while the rest of him was soaked through.

"Thank you."

He gave a brisk nod and turned to a nearby tree, yanking off his tattered shirt as he went.

Her mouth went dry all over again. Oh boy, he was built like a dream. Rippling muscles along his back, abs for days. She'd almost have believed a bodybuilder had saved her, except he was green. Did orcs have those kinds of competitions or was he just naturally buff?

He tossed the shirt away into a nearby thicket. He wasn't going to keep it? He was going to go shirtless from here on out? Was this some kind of reward or was it torture?

Then he flicked at the tips of the sharp branches on one of the bare trees. He picked one that was thick enough to be sturdy but tapered into a point. It was almost as tall as he was and the crack as he snapped it off at the trunk of the tree cut through the quiet and made her hands clench.

He wasn't staggering anymore, even over the rock laden beach. That had to be a good sign, right? Proof he was healed? The fading light was too dim for her to see if his complexion had recovered. He'd been so pale, he looked almost white. Like the inside of a cucumber or maybe a honeydew smoothie.

Her stomach twisted, unsure if she was hungry or about

to throw up. She really needed to stop comparing this guy to food.

The orc waded into the spring, holding the stick under his arm so both hands were free. The pool was so clear she could see his legs beneath until he got to where the water was bubbling. He cupped the liquid in his hands and rinsed his face clean.

Then he snorted, coughing and sputtering as if he'd inhaled it.

"Are you okay?" Miranda was poised to push her way off the boulder. She knew CPR. She could save him if he was drowning. God, after all that, don't let him fricking drown. She couldn't handle being out here alone with nothing but her own thoughts.

He cast her a harsh look. Those emerald eyes narrowed. Spitting the water out of his mouth, he wiped off with his arm and Miranda was embarrassed by the knowledge that, of *course*, he wasn't drowning. No one was stupid enough to breathe water out of their own palm.

It was fine. He was alive. Everything was okay.

But it wasn't.

Everyone was dead.

Miranda squeezed her eyes shut, rubbed at her knees, rocked back and forth as if the motion might ease the pressing agony gripping her chest.

Her babies were dead. Why hadn't she died with them?

How had she survived at all? She couldn't remember how she'd gotten out of the vault. Out of the vent. A whimper broke through her lips.

"Miranda."

Her name, spoken from that deep, rumbling voice, popped her right out of her torture.

He moved the stick into his hand and made his way to where the water was dark, though it only came up to the middle of his thigh. His green, muscular torso was starkly contrasted by the bright reds and yellows of the surrounding trees. Lord, he was built like a dream. It made total sense why she'd convinced herself he was one.

He narrowed his eyes at her before turning back to his task. He stopped next to a log jutting from the surface with the stick raised like a spear. Crisp water lapped around the damp, blackened wood. A breeze rustled the trees, moving the thinned-out leaves to let in the light of the setting sun so she could make out the planes of his face. He furrowed his brows in concentration as he peered below the surface of the water, as if he could somehow see beyond the ripples.

His arm moved so fast she couldn't even process it. The sound of a splash was the first sign he'd lunged at all. His makeshift spear rose from the depths to reveal three still wiggling fish.

Miranda froze, shifting between shock and something darker she didn't want to name. She was heavily dependent on this stranger. His threat of hunting her down if she fled rang harshly between her ears until it was deafening.

His eyes held her captive as he emerged from the water. His woolen slacks were now as soaked as his chest.

She worried her lip as he approached. "Are you cold? Here. Have your cloak back."

She'd startled him again. He was expecting her to comment on something else. She glanced at the fish. "That was really impressive. You could win all the prizes at the county fair. Do they have spearing competitions at the county fair? I never actually went to—"

"Miranda."

She loved how he said her name. There was a slight accent to it. A lingering rumble on the "r."

Mirrrh-anda.

He wrapped his hands around her waist again. His warm hands heated her ribs as he placed her gently on the ground.

She reached up to touch his forehead. It was reasonably cool. "Fever's gone."

He shook his head, eyes mirroring a deep well of bafflement she found adorable. Then he took back his cape and put it on. "We're going back to my pack."

"Okay," she murmured, taking his arm again. He was so much bigger than her. So much taller. A memory flushed her as they walked. "When I was a kid, I got lost in the grocery store. The caretaker had been watching ten of us girls all at once. I was really small back then and got overlooked."

He raised an incredulous brow.

"Okay," she amended, with a wry chuckle, "I guess I'm still small, but I bet everyone is small compared to you."

He huffed.

"Anyway. The store clerk let me hold his arm while he led me back to the group. Reminds me of this." She gave his arm a squeeze. It was hard as a rock, all muscle. "He wasn't as buff as you, not that I mind. Muscles are great. Makes me feel even safer."

"Even *safer*?"

Miranda looked up into the orc's face, blinking at his furrowed brow and wide eyes. She supposed it *was* strange to feel safe with him. She didn't know him. He was a complete stranger.

An alien stranger in the middle of the woods on a different planet.

Was this a different planet?

God, she was going to lose her dang mind.

He said nothing, and after a quick walk in growing darkness, they had returned to the clearing where they'd left his leather bag.

The orc—Govek, his name was Govek—peeled her off his arm slowly. She clenched her teeth to keep from arguing. Yes, he was a stranger. Yes, he was inhuman. Yes, he had enough muscles to potentially crush her into dust in one hit. But dang, she did *not* want him to leave her here. She'd rather take her chances with him than be left all alone.

She'd already lost *everything* else.

She squeezed her eyes shut, refusing to think about it.

The huge puddle she'd made while healing him was a few feet away and she trembled at the memory of her panic. The trembling quickly turned to shivers in the fading sunlight. Her eyes fixed on Govek as he searched his pack. Was he going to leave?

He pulled two small black stones from the pack and left her next to it. Gathering rocks into a circle in one of the dryer spots. He filled his little rock fort with damp leaves and wood. Then he struck the black stones against each other, the crack echoing into the night and showering sparks. His pile burst into flames like bacon on a barbecue.

She settled down in front of the fire, marveling. All her experiences had come from making bonfires in the summer at the group home. She remembered the staff needing to add more logs and sticks multiple times before a roaring blaze like this one was going.

Govek threw a few more damp logs on the fire, showering sparks into the night. Her gaze followed them as they rose high and dimmed away in the blackened sky, replaced by stars twinkling above the tree canopy. The scent of smoke was oddly comforting. After all she'd been through on Earth, she would have thought soot and ash were the last things she'd want to smell.

But there was something different about this wood smoke. Something . . . cleaner.

It wasn't laced with chemicals. She hugged her knees. Memories of Earth spiraling. Walking to work. Car exhaust. Processed soup for lunch. Cutting up artificially grown apples for the kids' snacks. Sticky little toddler hands.

Don't think about it. Don't think.

She heard a knife slicing through flesh, and it pulled her from her memory. The scent of fish.

Miranda forced her eyes open again and concentrated on the orc as he gutted the trout with practiced efficiency. He seemed to be using his fingers for the task. Where was the knife? She hadn't found one in is pack but maybe that was what cut her?

He'd almost died. And she would have been the last one left alive again.

Her stomach rolled, and she forced a few deep breaths, willing the panic to ebb. He was *fine* now.

His distance was respectful, but she wished he would come closer, wished he would talk more, wished he would help distract her from the pressing weight gripping her chest, threatening to smother her.

"You don't have to cook those if you don't want to. I've always liked sushi."

Govek glanced up from his task, but still said nothing.

"Well," Miranda amended. "I guess I usually ate the precooked stuff. Real raw fish was so expensive. Like, a hundred and fifty dollars for one roll. I never had that kind of money. But I think the inexpensive stuff was just as good."

Miranda paused her jabbering as Govek finished cleaning the fish and brought them back to his makeshift spear. Skewering them evenly before setting them over the fire.

"I hope this lives up to your expectations," he said.

"I'm sure it will. I'm hungry enough that I would eat anything. Er . . . sorry, that came out wrong. I'm sure your fish will be wonderful. I'm super grateful you're making them. Thank you. Really."

His furrowed brow softened, and he gave a nod.

"How are you feeling?" Miranda asked.

"I am fully healed," he replied, turning the fish over the fire.

"By water magic," she breathed.

"Yes."

She glanced down at the minor cut on her hand she'd gotten when searching through his things. "It only works on you?"

"The spring is of the Fades. It was an ancient gift from them to the sentinels of the Surface."

"Sentinels of the Surface? I thought you said you were an orc."

"My species is orc. My duty is to be a sentinel. We protect Faeda and it protects us in return."

Faeda. A different planet. She started combing nervously through her matted hair.

"Where is your village?" Govek finally asked.

She hesitated, considering her responses. "Uh . . . in Washington state?"

His forehead furrowed deep, casting dark shadows over

his eyes.

"In America?"

Still nothing.

Her breath hitched, but she managed past the lump in her throat. "On . . . planet Earth?"

He really was an alien.

Which meant she was now too.

Her heartbeat picked up speed, did double time, hard enough she could feel it in her fingertips.

He turned back to the fish, his expression grim. Apparently, he needed space to process, just like she did.

The comforting crackle of the fire continued to soothe her, and the lingering smoke drowned out the final remaining traces of her post-apocalyptic hell. She wished the smoke could cleanse her memories just as easily.

Miranda's eyes pricked harshly as the face of Mr. Barker swam into her vision. He was by far the nicest boss she'd ever had.

She'd only worked at Blackridge Bank for two months, but in that time, she could tell Mr. Barker truly cared about all the tellers. He always went out of his way to stock the break room with snacks, approve vacations without question, and joke around to lighten the mood. His laugh lines and frizzy white hair flashed through her mind's eye.

He'd been the last human she'd ever seen.

Miranda would never get an explanation from him. He never told her why he'd shoved her into the vault alone. She should hate him for what his hasty action had put her through. Or thank him for saving her life in such a ruthless way. Instead, the agony of grief gripped around her heart so fiercely it was physical pain.

Liquid heat dripped down her cheeks as her thoughts

turned to her other job. Riverside Daycare Center, where she spent her evenings and mornings.

She thought of all her babies, whose lives had been cut tragically short.

She hadn't been there to save them.

"Eat."

The growling demand was harsh and broke the bubble of her sorrow so easily it almost made her gasp. Something about this male's voice threw her out of her thoughts and brought her back to reality.

This reality. Not the one she'd suffered on Earth.

She blinked down at the roasted fish—crispy skin and delicious steam assaulted her senses. She took the branch he'd used to skewer it for cooking with trembling fingers and ventured a bite, uncaring of bones or scales.

It melted in her mouth like butter. Fresh and exquisite. It wasn't as if she hadn't had fish before, but this was different. Clean. Pure. It had never touched a single drop of polluted water in its brief life.

She ate half of it before she realized the orc was watching her in muted horror. She gulped down the bite she had in her mouth and felt her cheeks heat. She had eaten the bones in her haste.

"How long has it been since you ate?"

"I had the bread you . . ." She stopped when she saw his harsh scowl. Fiddling with the crispy front fin of the fish, she noticed she hadn't gotten to its head yet. Thank god. If he was so shocked at her eating the bony tail, she couldn't imagine how he might have responded to her sucking down its skull like a vacuum.

"A couple days," she admitted.

A low growl sounded, and she yelped as he jerked the

fish out of her grasp. In her panic to keep the food, she snapped, "Give it back!"

He didn't, and he was so much bigger than her, holding her off easily with nothing more than his elbow. She watched in dismay as he ripped her meal apart and gathered up the tiny pieces on a large yellow leaf.

"You cannot eat the bones. You will choke on them."

She paused in her attempts to reach over him, startled at his misplaced concern. "No, I won't."

"You will."

"My throat isn't that small."

"Yes, it is."

"I assure you it's big enough to handle anything you want to put down it," she stated before she could think better of it.

He froze for a heavy minute before a shudder raked over him, and his eyes snapped to hers. He looked as if he wanted to swallow *her* whole.

She was in way over her head, but she'd watched enough raunchy movies to know that flirting could get you a lot of places, and she would literally do anything to win her fish back.

Govek huffed and slid the leaf over to sit on her knee. "Don't do that."

She mumbled innocently. "Do what?"

"Tempt me. You know not what you ask for."

Sure, she did. She might have *technically* been a virgin, but she certainly wasn't innocent. Twenty-second century Earth was about as prudish as a pop star and sex toys were as easy to come by as candy bars.

But, as the male heaved heavy breaths, as his enormous muscles bunched and his scowl darkened his features, she realized she probably shouldn't be provoking him. Even if that provocation would lead to a very pleasurable distraction from her current turmoil.

Halfway through these randy thoughts she noticed she'd already eaten all the fish he'd given her and was about to lick the leaf clean. Maybe even break down and eat the dang leaf, too.

Govek plopped another pile down before she could lift it and she went back to eating without a word. Then he handed her some water. "Slow sips."

She supposed she should obey for now. She didn't want to upchuck all the fish.

She was partway through the third or fourth "plate" before her stomach became full enough for her to acknowledge that the orc wasn't eating anything. "What about you?" If she could polish off three small trout, Govek could probably eat thirty.

"I am fine."

"But you're hurt." She trailed off, remembering he actually wasn't hurt anymore. She gulped, fiddled with the fragrant flakes of meat she had left. "Sorry. I went a little crazy there, huh?"

"You were starving."

"It's only been a couple of days."

He growled. "You look fragile enough that a stiff breeze would blow you away like dandelion fluff."

A puff of laughter bubbled up from her full stomach, forcing a smile to stretch her chapped lips. "You have dandelions here too? I guess I can believe it. Those weeds were so prolific they would spread to different planets, wouldn't they?"

The orc's face softened as he watched her. The usual

scowl vanished. She rested her head on her knees. Warm from the fire. Drowsy from the food.

"You should rest," he moved the leafy leftovers aside. Then he took off his cloak again, placed it on the ground next to the fire. "You may sleep here."

"Where will you sleep?" she asked, though she was already moving to lie down on it. He wouldn't be able to leave without his cloak, right?

"I'm fine," he said, throwing a few more logs on the fire.

"But—"

He shot her a look harsh enough to burn. Without another word, she settled down, exhaustion flattening her. "Okay."

He snorted with what she assumed was approval.

"You won't leave, right?" She couldn't help herself.

But he answered readily. "No. I will not leave."

A shudder rolled over her and she willed tears not to fall. She had no choice but to believe him. She took a deep breath of the rich smoky pine scent of his cloak and took a long look up at the billions of stars twinkling above her.

With their light shining upon her face, Miranda succumbed to sleep.

SIX

GOVEK

Govek watched the mysterious woman fall into a restless slumber. Her sleep drunk movements were jerky, and her brow was furrowed.

She dreamed of terrors. Of that, he was certain. He warred between the driving instinct to offer her comfort and the burning need to let her rest.

She'd saved his life. Fuck.

He wrenched his hand through his hair, tugging hard enough to rip strands free. Her imprint was thrumming like violent currents through his veins. It would be fucking agony to dispel it. Far worse than it had been with Yerina.

But he must. He could not keep this woman. He was going to *war*.

She mumbled something in her sleep, causing Govek to tense, to come to attention. Her voice was a beautiful melody. So high and sweet. He hung off her every breath.

"Don't leave," she muttered into the cloak.

Guilt speared him. It was like she could read his blasted mind.

But she would be fine on her own. He couldn't be sure what kind of world this "Earth" was, but judging from her condition and her babble about dogs, she had evaded predators and knew how to survive. She even had that vile tincture that had torn his nose to pieces. It was probably what had saved her when she was running to the spring and back.

He'd been careful not to take a strong whiff of her since he'd healed himself in the spring. Even though every stupid fiber of his worthless being craved to do so. She was still doused in the noxious fumes.

They would protect her when he was gone.

She'd saved his life, and in return, he would abandon her.

His wretched claws crept out from beneath his nails, digging into his palms. He let out a harsh growl so deep it rumbled his entire chest.

Then he froze, whipping his head toward Miranda. He found her more relaxed than before, her expression more peaceful. Thank Fades, he hadn't woken her.

She looked fucking wrung. The circles around her massive brown eyes were so dark they looked like bruises. Eyes that were so expressive it left him no illusion to her emotions. When she smiled, it felt like the warmth of summer and the little laugh she'd gifted him was—

Fuck. *Fuck.* He was leaving her tomorrow.

Even if he *wanted* to keep her, he had nothing to offer. No boons to win her over.

Yerina had liked furs and fruits, but these Fades-forsaken woods outside the Rove Tree's reach had been abandoned by all animals except for blighted predators and half-starved hares. The summer fruits had been picked over ages ago. Fish was the only sustainable food.

He might be able to find a few herbs if he looked hard enough—and got terribly lucky.

He would never be able to earn her affections with such meager offerings. He let out another frustrated growl.

Miranda made a humming sound, and he froze again. He'd woken her?

No. She was still asleep, and he sagged with relief.

Her admission about his growls feeling "tingly" broke into his thoughts. Never had any being described his threatening sounds as such. She'd rubbed her hand along her chest, right between the lush globes of her breasts.

And now she wasn't even wearing a fucking shirt.

He ground his teeth and stared into the fire until his eyes burned from the smoke.

Miranda's whimpering broke through his determination to ignore her.

She seemed to be having another nightmare.

Blast this imprint and its ruthless demands. He fixed his eyes on the woman.

His woman.

A shiver of pleasure crept up his spine as he clenched his fingers in his hair. His control was slipping. Another particularly pitiful cry forced him to his knees and brought him forward to her side.

"Hush," he murmured. But she didn't obey him. He hadn't expected her to. His voice wasn't created to bring comfort.

It was meant to terrify.

Tears gathered around her long, dark lashes and her pink lips trembled.

"Shh," he managed to make the sound soft and quiet.

The tear broke free and slid down her cheek. She let out a whimper that bellowed through his frame and the imprint roared with blazing agony. He could not withhold a growl of frustration.

And in response, her body relaxed. Her expression smoothed, her tears stopped, and her limbs went limp.

Because he had *growled*?

What he would give to read her mind now. To get inside her head. The imprint in his chest thrummed its fire, but could not reveal what his woman was thinking. It only made his blood blister with the longing to do so.

If she liked his growling, should he do it more?

No. *No!* It was illogical. Went against the nature of all living things. *He* should haunt her nightmares.

It must be a coincidence. Well placed timing.

He raked a hand through his hair and watched her intently.

She buried her nose in his cloak, tucking her full lips against it, and sucked a deep breath into her lungs. "Smells good," she mumbled, all sleep-drunk perfection. "Govek . . ."

Oh *fuck*.

He trembled, pleasure shuddering down his spine and spiking heat through him as goosebumps broke out over his arms. Fuck, fuck, *fuck*. He needed to get out of here. Go back to the spring. Douse the fire in his blood.

Her hand reached out and took his, and his heart skittered up into his throat. He fixed his eyes on her face, waiting for her own eyes to open. Waiting for her to admit that she'd been awake this whole time. That she'd been pulling some sort of cruel farce because, of *course*, she wouldn't be attracted to him. Of course, she wouldn't find him appealing or comforting. He was loathsome, vile, unable to control—

Her body went completely boneless, and her face sagged into a deep sleep.

While holding his fucking hand. With his claws *right there*.

Govek tried to pull away, but her brow furrowed slightly when he did and he knew the instant he ripped free of her she would wake. She would wake and he would be faced with her barely covered body, her sweet voice, and her incredible scent, and those lovely brown eyes—all bright and perfect.

He was an imbecile. He had to let her go. He was going to *war*.

But for tonight . . . for now, he could enjoy this.

Govek curled up then, finding a position in which he could relax while she still gripped him. He allowed his thoughts to grow heavy. He'd almost died today. Boar, wolves, poison . . .

He fell unconscious with the heavy knowledge that this woman had saved him multiple times.

A SHARP GASP instantly brought him out of slumber. The dim light of morning assaulted his dreary gaze.

There was a pressure against his palm, a scramble, and finally, a sudden chill.

The woman. She'd let him go and left him.

Blast! The sleep had done her a great service. Her eyes were bright and her coloring had returned, bringing a subtle pink to her cheeks and lips. She was a welcome sight.

"Y-you're real."

A heavy sigh escaped him as he took in their surroundings. There didn't seem to be any predators about, though most were not stupid enough to threaten an orc. The day would be clear once the morning fog burned away.

He would make good time on his way to the Warlord.

"O-oh gosh. God. Sorry." Miranda pressed a palm to her forehead. "I'm just . . . all out of it. I . . . I'm . . ." She paused, seemed to be distracted, staring up at the trees again. The brambles and thickets. Reverence and confusion. This expression had fallen over her features many times the day before, and Govek was uncertain if he would ever grow accustomed to it.

He reached for his pack and sifted through it, making difficult choices over what he wanted to keep and what he would send with his female.

The female. Fuck.

She gulped hard. "Are you okay? How do you feel?"

"I am fine," Govek snapped, getting to his feet. He was stiff from being in the same position for so long.

"Wow. You really are green."

He snorted, wryly amused.

"W-what are you again? An orc?"

"Yes."

"Okay." She took deep breaths. "Okay, okay."

She wandered off a few paces, shivering. The vile urge to offer his own cloak to her bellowed in him. He went to her pack instead, abandoned near the fire. It had almost nothing in it. The crisp blue was haunting against the soil and the slick texture was like nothing he'd ever touched before.

This woman was not his mystery to solve. This is where they would part ways.

He shoved her pack into his own, determined to forget it ever existed and held his belongings out to her. "Take this."

She hesitated, and then hefted the bag onto her shoulder. Its weight strained her and his heart thundered as if trying to work against his own mind.

He gestured to the west, calculating how fast she might travel. "Two days' walk and you will come across Baytton." He hoped Baytton was still there. Rove Wood Clan had no contact with human villages outside of Oakwall. Tavggol had been working tirelessly to build peaceful trade with another, only to have his plans go up in deadly, horrific smoke.

Smoke that had choked out his life far too soon.

Govek fisted his claws so his female would not see them and set about extinguishing what remained of the fire. "Baytton is a human village and has high walls. You will be safe there."

"You . . . you're . . . what?"

She was shaking more violently now, and Govek tried not to look at her. His instinct to aid her was shrill. "As long as you do not mention to the Waking Order you were in the company of an orc, they will welcome you." Better yet. "Or tell them you found me poisoned and finished me off. Stole my belongings." They may question her about his clan and the whereabouts of his body, but not harshly.

"No," she said as he dug handfuls of damp soil and threw them onto the embers. They sizzled and popped in protest before going out with a final puff of smoke.

"You can't . . . I won't let you . . . you can't just *leave* me here."

His gut pitched. These woods were deadly. Hundreds of creatures larger than her stalked within. But he could not bring her with him to Karthoc's forge, and he certainly could not venture anywhere near a human village. Soldiers of the Waking Order patrolled for tens of leagues outside the walls.

"You will be fine."

She would be. *She* wasn't the one who was going to have to fight off an imprint that shouldn't even exist to begin with. She wouldn't be raked with agony every step she took away from him. *She* wouldn't have a burning urge to return to his side, despite all logic and reason.

But he'd broken off Yerina's imprint. He could break Miranda's too.

"Use that tincture you have to hide your scent," he told her.

"Govek, *no.* I want to go with you."

A shiver stirred within him at her plea. It broke down several barriers he'd been trying to erect between them. "My path takes me through perilous lands. You will perish in the attempt."

"I can make it."

He shot her a harsh look. "I assure you, you will not." She was skin and bones, and she didn't even have proper clothes.

"Could . . . could you take me to the village then?"

Was she trying to lure him to his death? Flames licked the edges of his mind. "You think me foolish enough to risk being slaughtered by the Waking Order to ensure your safety?"

"What is the Waking Order?"

The honest query speared him, made his throat dry.

"Washington state, in America, on planet Earth."

His stomach clenched, and he chose his next words carefully. "They are a human sect who ignorantly believe my kind, and all sentinels, must be eradicated. Should they see me, they will slaughter me on sight. Or worse, torture me for information about my clan. I will be flayed alive and cooked on a spit."

His forehead broke into a sweat as he fought back foul memories. Gruesome sights that had torn through him.

Of what remained of his brother in the Clairton town square.

Of the blood and the stench and the battle rage.

Of the madness and destructive magic he'd been unable to control.

Gentle fingers smoothed over his arm, and he flinched, reeling from her sudden touch.

Miranda stood with her brown eyes beseeching and her voice warbling. "Please take me with you."

He took harsh, gulping breaths. "Move west, follow the sun, and you will encounter humans."

"Please, Govek."

He closed his eyes against the driving urge to obey.

"I just . . . I can't be alone right now. I won't slow you down, I promise."

Her pleading was nearly his undoing. He barely rasped. "I am going to *war*, Miranda."

She flinched as if he had slapped her and the terror rendering her expression to pieces gripped like a vise in his chest. "War?"

"Yes."

"You're at war?"

He could only nod.

"B-but you can't be. This can't be. I'm not . . . I can't . . ." Her voice raked over his flesh like a harsh winter chill, scraping against his senses.

His gaze shot to her hand, where her fingers were digging into the cut on her palm. Breaking it open anew. Bright blood dripped from between her fingers onto the forest floor, painting the decaying leaves at her feet. "Stop!"

The slice of a yowl drowned away his order.

A saber cat.

The beast pounced toward Miranda with deadly precision.

Nervous energy burst through Govek's limbs. He shot out, shoving her behind him, and threw himself toward the cat's gaping maw.

Govek's fist collided with the animal's thick skull. It cracked, and the cat plummeted to the forest floor.

He looked back at his woman long enough to find her scrambling to her feet. His heavy bag had pulled her down.

The cat snarled and Govek whirled, bracing his feet. Its jaws were dripping, its sharp teeth were tinted black. Its eyes were glazed and listless. Its movements were jerky and unpredictable.

It had the blight.

The cat charged with ruthless precision, claws digging into the ground, snapping and spitting. It shot *around* him.

Toward Miranda.

He roared, leaping into the air and tackled it. It scrambled and flailed and screamed into the foggy air. It was all he could do to avoid its deadly claws.

Its neck was right there. With a quick assessment of his

woman, he flashed his eyes and found Miranda still horrified, and he fucking *couldn't do it*. He could not risk terrorizing her with the sight of him ripping the creature's throat out with his own vile fangs.

The hesitation caused the cat to break free.

Miranda did the unthinkable. She bolted for the woods.

The cat whipped toward his woman. Its instinct to chase its prey making it inconceivably fast as it hurtled after Miranda.

Panic speared his mind, and he shot his hand out, caught the tail of the cat and crushed it in his grip. It snapped. The bones wrenched apart under the force of stopping the beast from hurtling toward Miranda.

But the flesh held.

The cat screamed and spat in agony, writhing and twisting around to skewer him. Govek's own terror went higher and gave him precision. He dragged it back, dodged its claws, and pushed his knee into its ribs until they crunched under his weight.

Anguish roared to life in his bones. The cat's tortured cries grated his senses, and he gnashed his teeth against the guilt that he was causing it such pain.

It whipped its head around, its teeth snapping so close to his cheek he felt its spittle on his face and smelled its rotten breath. Govek wrapped his hand around its neck and sliced clean through the fur and tissues. Blood sprayed in an arc against the ground. It was dead in an instant.

Rage roared to life within him, and he lurched toward the trees where Miranda had run. He would hunt her. Force her to return. Make her face the torture her stupidity had caused this creature.

Had caused him.

She'd fucking *ran.*

Just like Yerina.

His chest burned.

"A-are you okay?"

He froze, eyes darting. Miranda was staggering *toward* him. But she had run. She'd—

"Oh god! Your hand. Here."

She was so close to him. Right in front. Her fingers were soft as they grazed his wrist. Thank Fades he'd managed to sheath his claws already.

His mind caught up with him and he shook his head, forced the agony of her betrayal to dim.

This wasn't like Yerina. There was no comparison. Miranda had been fleeing for her life and Yerina had been scorning him.

He squeezed his eyes shut in an attempt to block out the pain of his former woman's abandonment.

She dumped the water pouch out over his hand, rubbing it clean. Moving it around.

Searching for injuries?

"You're okay. You're okay," she murmured half to herself. She was terrified.

Terrified *for* him. Not *of* him.

Govek did not know how to process this interaction, so he went still, allowing his woman to flutter her soft fingers over his flesh.

"It's . . . it . . ." Her eyes were flooded with tears and her face was pale. "It was screaming."

Govek gulped. Taking a deep calming breath, he came down from his raging. Found reason. "It is past its pain."

She sniffled piteously, staring at the cat's lifeless body. "It's so pretty. I'm sorry. I shouldn't have run."

He wanted to tell her it was blighted. That it would have died, anyway. That the few agonies it had suffered at his hands were nothing compared to what it would have had to endure as it rotted away from the inside.

But another dreadful thought spiked in his system and drowned out his ability to speak.

He could not leave her alone in the woods.

Miranda would die. She would be picked off by a predator or injured by her own misstep. Likely only moments after she left his sight.

But he certainly could not take her to war with him.

He did not know what to do. Where would they go from here?

Fuck the Fades for giving her to him. For dropping her into his lap. They had been cruel to him for the bulk of his miserable life, and this was just one more blasted misfortune he would have to endure.

"Govek?" Her gentle, sorrow-laced tone was maddening. He willed her to be silent even as he swallowed the temptation to order her to say his name so sweetly again.

"Can you walk?" he whispered, glancing at her trembling knees. He did not wait for a reply. Instead, he lugged his discarded pack over his shoulder before scooping the woman off her feet.

She was so light it staggered him, but her frame was warm and supple against his bare chest. He relished the sensation, gulped as it soothed him. He tucked her into the crook of his arm as she squeaked with surprise.

"Where are we going?" she asked as he carted her off into the depths of the forest in the opposite direction of any human settlements.

He did not answer her—because he did not know.

CHAPTER

SEVEN

MIRANDA

E arth was gone, and Miranda had landed in a whole other kind of death trap.

For a brief, horrific moment, she understood why humans had hunted predators into extinction. That wild cat had been vicious, terrifying.

She did *not* know how to fight something like that. She'd barely survived the dogs.

"Th-thank you for saving me," she whispered, trying to fight the rolling in her stomach. Govek held her firmly against his chest and walked carefully through the forest. His eyes were dark and brooding as they ventured deeper into the unknown.

She would die if he abandoned her now, and she suspected, after what had just happened, after what a bumbling, panicky idiot she'd been, he was very close to doing just that.

"I swear I won't . . ." Won't what? Be a burden? She already was.

She'd only traveled in Earth's apocalyptic nightmare for a few days, and she'd almost died. She had absolutely no skills to help him. None.

Her chin trembled. Earth was *gone,* and she had no idea what to do now.

"Stop."

The harsh growl dried her tears before they could fall. Something about the low rumble of Govek's tone was so soothing it made her forget how desperate things were and drowned out the horrors that kept lurking in the back of her mind.

She didn't want him to leave her.

The silence between them continued for a few long minutes while Govek carried her. His frame was warm, but tense. The chattering of birds and the whistling of the wind brought little comfort.

Earth had lots of birds before the war had gotten really bad.

And this world was at war, too.

How could she be dropped out of one cataclysm only to land in another? Was she doomed to watch multiple worlds be ravaged by carnage and strife? Was she paying some universal price for the atrocities humanity had committed on Earth?

"Stop, woman."

She was ripped out of Govek's warmth and plunked down on hard stone so quickly it jarred her out of her madness. Her eyes strained to find Govek ripping her fingers away from the wound on her palm. It was twice as big as it had been originally. Blood dripped down her wrist.

His angry mutters somehow calmed her. He was brutal and irritable, but the harsh emotions helped stabilize her.

He pulled a vial from the pack and poured it over the cut. It felt icy cold, but she kept her hand limp as he worked. The wound closed in an instant, leaving only a thin red line. Her mouth popped open. "Was that magic? That was magic, wasn't it? Wow! That's amazing! It's really gone. I thought that magic didn't work on humans."

"The spring doesn't, but orcs have their own tinctures that do." He arranged things inside his bag. "I have only a few."

Guilt gnawed at her. "Thank you. You didn't have to waste it on me."

"Just don't do it again."

She wanted to ask why he cared so much, but was afraid of the answer. Afraid that pointing it out would make him realize he *didn't* have a reason to be nice to her.

"Here." He held out the water pouch and didn't force her to slow down this time. Granted, she was a lot less frantic, working stiff gulps down her parched throat. Her tongue no longer felt like sandpaper, but her teeth were still a little gritty.

She looked up toward the bright, cloudless sky. Her breath fogged as she asked, "You said this world was called Faeda?"

"Yes," he said, taking the pouch from her grip.

"It's perfect." She looked down again, to the wet ground and the rotting leaves. "What was that animal called? The one that attacked us?"

"Saber cat."

She nodded, gulping. "I'm sorry it died."

"It had the blight," Govek said harshly, but his words comforted her, nonetheless. "It needed to be culled."

"What is the blight?"

"An illness wrought by the Fades. The cat would have succumbed to its affliction eventually."

Miranda kept her eyes lowered, fixed them on those odd, spiral leaves, thinking over the events which were much less of a blur now that her adrenaline had ebbed. "But it wouldn't have suffered if I hadn't run. You wouldn't have had to grab its tail like that and . . ."

"No."

Her breath shuddered, and she met his eyes. "I . . . I won't run like that again. I promise."

Govek said nothing, but his eyes flashed with something like surprise.

She wanted to ask if she could stay with him. Make him swear he wouldn't leave her to fend for herself in the forest, but it wasn't a fair request. She knew she was a liability.

Miranda, desperate for a distraction from her rounding thoughts, pointed to the spiral leaves in the muck. "What tree are those from?"

"That is from an oak born from the Great Rove Tree. One of the Fades' Relics."

"That's not what oaks look like on Earth," she said, referring more to how vibrant this Faeda tree was than the spiral leaf shape. "The Fades are your gods?"

"Yes."

Earth had so many dang religions, Miranda couldn't even fathom them all. In Earth's ancient times, before lack of food became more important, humans often had wars over their religions. "Is . . . is your war because of them?"

Govek was silent, and Miranda met his gaze. His eyes

skittered away, his hand dragged over his scalp, pulling his hair.

"The Waking Order," he said slowly, "has deemed sentinels to be the cause of the blight and seeks our eradication. They also believe our demise will wake the Fades from their slumber and bring a new era."

So, yes then. "All sentinels are orcs?"

"Orcs for the surface, goblins for the structure, and sylphs for the sky. All three races are sentinels to the Fades."

Her lips thinned. "And the Waking Order are humans who are causing the war?"

His ragged sigh doused any hope she might have scraped together. "Yes."

Miranda sagged, defeated, completely unsurprised. "Obviously it would be humans. Who else?"

The gentle breeze continued, but it didn't cool her. Of *course,* he wouldn't be keen on bringing her along. She was from the race his kind were at war with.

If he was going to leave her here, she might as well let him get to it.

"I'm sorry," she said, meeting his eyes with as much gumption as she could muster. "If . . . if you want to leave me here, it's okay. I'll figure it out."

He searched her face for what felt like an eternity. "You want me to leave?"

"No," she said with a wry laugh. "God, no. I'll probably . . ." she trailed off, not wanting to make him feel guilty with the truth that she'd likely get picked off by another saber cat the second he was out of sight.

Or maybe not. She'd been stupid lucky so far.

Miraculously. She shouldn't even be alive right now. She should have died with the rest of Earth.

But she hadn't. She'd made it here. And nothing said she couldn't survive Faeda too.

Govek was still crouching before her, his body tense, his eyes pensive. His hands were in tight fists, resting on his knees.

Miranda reached out and clasped them. Stroked her thumbs along his knuckles, met his wide, shocked eyes. "We're even now. We've both saved each other. I know I'm useless to you, especially if you're going to war. If you tell me how to get to that village, I'll be fine on my own. Really."

Everything seemed to still—the birds, the wind, even her heart.

And then Govek snarled, "No."

His eyes fixed on her hands, and she gripped him tighter. Half of her hoped he would unfurl his fists and let her take them, and the other expected him to rip away from her.

"I have proclaimed you as my conquest," he said firmly, determined. He leaned in closer, the heat of his body soaked through the cloak. "I will not let you go."

She licked her lips. A million questions blurring through her head. What was a conquest? Where would they go now? What could she do to ensure he wouldn't change his mind? She was afraid to ask any of them.

He snapped his gaze to hers again. "If you flee, I will hunt you, Miranda. So, I suggest you come willingly."

Hoo boy, was she willing! His voice was that sultry low rumble that made her mind turn to mush, and suddenly, she wanted to run just to find out what hunting her entailed.

She'd run from him and her memories of Earth at the same time. See which one would catch her first.

"If you desire to be of use, simply continue your chatter."

Her eyes widened. "Continue my chatter?"

Govek went tense but grumbled. "Your voice is pleasant."

His warmth was making her dizzy. "You like my voice?" As much as she liked his? "Well, chattering at you is something I can handle." She shot him a giddy smile, delighted by his admission. "I've been told by a few people I talk too much. Anything else you want me to handle?"

His eyes widened and Miranda realized far too late what she'd insinuated, but she wasn't about to take it back. Even as she grappled with the fact that he was a completely different species from her.

But he wasn't *that* different. Not really. She focused on his large hands under hers. They were built the same. Five fingers. Opposable thumbs. Knuckles and nails. His pinky had untucked from his fist, revealing the long, black claw. She reached out to touch it.

And it shot back into his hand.

Miranda gasped and gripped his hand for a better look. He jerked, wrenching his hands away, and barreled to his feet in shock.

Her eyes were still on his hand, which was now back to black, blunted nails.

"You have retractable claws?"

"I will not harm you."

"Can I see them?" she asked, fascinated.

"What?" The word came out strangled, almost a wheeze.

"Can I see your hand?" She'd seen characters in movies with retractable claws like that but had never dreamed it could be a reality.

He hesitated and drew in a long breath. "You need not concern yourself. I will not harm you with them."

"I didn't think you would. It's just cool."

Confusion furrowed his brow, and his shoulders relaxed. "Cool? Are you cold?"

A little snort of laughter left her lips. "No, no. I meant interesting. Neat. I want to see them closer. Will you let me?"

Govek hesitated, thinking. Then he kneeled down on one knee. He was so big, even in this position. He examined her face for another moment, as if looking for any hint of anxiety, or perhaps trying to hide away his own.

He held up his left hand and slowly extended the claws.

They appeared like pointed acrylics, if acrylics were as sharp as surgical blades, jet black, and were around two inches long.

She carefully took his hand and heard his breath hitch, but she ignored it. His claws came from underneath his actual fingernails. The space between his fingertip and first knuckle was long enough to accommodate them.

"Can you retract?"

He huffed and obliged. They disappeared into his hands, and only a slight indent showed against his green skin. She traced the indent. There was a slight difference in firmness. "Does it hurt?"

"What?"

Miranda looked up at his bewildered expression and wished she had a camera so she could immortalize it. It made him look almost soft. Cute. "I mean, what would happen if your hand got crushed? Would they cut you from the inside?"

He flinched his head back slightly, blinking. "Woman, I suspect if my hands were crushed, I would be more worried about my bones than my claws."

She quirked a smile. "Probably." She tipped his hand over and placed hers to his. It was twice the size of her own. In fact, his torso, as a whole, seemed to be disproportionately larger than his lower half.

She amended that while it was disproportionate to the ratios a human male would have, she didn't know what the orc standards were.

His skin was smooth and varied in green hues, the knuckles being darker than the surrounding flesh, his palms were much lighter, with many nearly white calluses. She drifted her fingers up to his wrists, to the bulge of his muscled forearms.

"Miranda," his voice was breathy, almost a warning. She looked up at his face to make sure he was okay with this and found him a little apprehensive.

His ears were pointed, but sat close enough to his head that she wouldn't have noticed if she wasn't looking. She reached up to trace the tip without thinking and made him shudder.

"Sorry," she whispered. He didn't respond. Didn't tell her no. She brushed at his hair next. It was short and disheveled, having dried every which way. She scooted closer and found that it wasn't black, but an extremely dark shade of green. She trailed her fingers down his temples to frame his face.

His eyes went wider. The color was striking. Bright green with golden flecks. His pupils were dilated and almost swallowed the color up. She pressed her thumbs into his cheeks, finding them devoid of any stubble as well. In fact, his whole body was hairless. There wasn't any on his arms or chest.

She brushed a finger along the crooked break in his nose. "What happened?"

His jaw ticked before he managed, "I got it during my trial."

"Your trial?" Had he done something illegal? Did they even have that kind of structure here?

"Into adulthood. I took down a great boar. I kept this boon as proof."

A broken nose was a prize? She sat back to examine it. "It does give you some rugged charm."

His scowl deepened, and his eyes blinked rapidly, as if her compliment confused him.

She gripped his face again and narrowed in on the little tusks at his lower jaw, teasing her fingers along the bottom of his chin. He was so tense it seemed almost painful.

"We should leave, Miranda."

She blinked at his mouth as he snapped it shut. His tension heightened. She was certain he was about to spring away.

She wrapped her hands around the back of his skull and scratched lightly at his hairline, hoping it was as sensitive on him as it was on her.

He huffed. His jaw slacked slightly, enough to intrigue her. There was something odd about it. She continued scratching with one hand and moved her other up to tap at the tooth butting out from his lower lip.

"It's blunt?"

"I've . . . filed it." He sounded breathless now. As she

continued scratching, his muscles released. His relaxation deepened.

She grinned at her newfound power as his eyes shut.

"Do your teeth grow continuously or do you just get the one?"

He blinked several times before his eyes opened. "Uh . . . both."

Both? "Will you show me?"

He straightened. "No."

"Why?"

"You will be frightened."

She quirked her head, pursed her lips. "I don't think I will. I'm pretty relaxed."

"Let us keep it that way."

Miranda slid her other hand to the back of his head and dug her fingers into the base of his skull, pressing slow circles. He exhaled a strangled sound as she moved toward his forehead.

Much more of this and he would turn to putty in her hands and she grinned at the new power this gave her. She softened her touch at his temples. The short, coarse hairs framing his brow tickled her palms. His eyes closed, his shoulders slumped, his hands were limp at his sides.

His jaw was still tense. It had been tense the entire time she had been with him, and she was going to figure out why. Right now.

She moved her massaging fingers down to where his jaw hinged into his skull and pushed into it. "Flex for me?"

His tense muscles gave as he adjusted them so she could get better access to the deeper tissues.

His chin relaxed and fell further. And further. *And further*.

Her own jaw slacked as his mouth opened, moving like he was chewing.

Lord almighty! Did he have *teeth!*

He'd been hiding them. The slit of his mouth was wide, allowing him to cover his upper lip with his lower jaw. It couldn't have been comfortable for such a long period.

The tusks were the longest by far. Probably three inches total, but they were flanked by two much sharper looking teeth. The top fangs mirrored this pattern, but were smaller and inset slightly so they would fit together when he closed his mouth.

They were distinctly predatory. Obviously designed to rip out the throats of his victims. They shimmered from his saliva. The tips of the upper teeth were so sharp she felt like she'd be cut from looking at them. Only the largest tusks had been filed, and probably only because they were long enough to skewer him in the cheek if he flexed his jaw the wrong way.

She sat back slightly, taking it all in, and her heart flipped over.

By god, he looked *way* better. His face was no longer squat and rounded. She hadn't realized how odd his features were until she saw them as they were supposed to be. His cheeks were slender, not plump, his chin was long, not tight and bunched, his lower lip was less taut, and his upper one was full, whereas before it had been nonexistent.

His proportions were striking perfection, even with the slight under-bite, which wasn't nearly as pronounced now that his jaw was in the right spot.

He wasn't human, not at all, but dang, he was *gorgeous.*

She accidentally stopped rubbing him. His eyes popped open, and he reared away, scrambling to his feet. Her fingers caught on some of his hair, and it yanked free, making her flinch.

"Oh, god. Sorry. You okay?" she asked.

He was facing away from her, stalking toward the depths of the woods. For a terrifying moment, she thought he may be about to abandon her.

She scrambled up after him and gripped the edge of his cloak. His eyes went huge, as if he couldn't believe she would approach him of her own will. "I . . . I'm really sorry for pulling your hair out. Are you all right?"

He turned finally. His pupils were small pinpricks in those oceans of shimmering green. There was no anger in the set of his brows, however, and she breathed a desperate sigh of relief.

She reached up slowly and traced the frame of his face. He shuddered almost violently. Was he scared? It was unbelievable that this massive, powerful man could be scared of anything, and yet his expression betrayed him. "You don't have to do that."

His brows pinched in silent question.

"Hide your teeth. It looks uncomfortable."

And weird. Now that she'd seen what his face was supposed to look like, he seemed deformed with his jaw all crunched up.

"I do not want to frighten you," he said slowly, as his fingers curled around her wrist. "I do not want you to flee."

"I'm not going to flee." She had nowhere to go. "You've saved my life. Why would I run?"

He still hesitated, as if he didn't quite believe her.

"If you were going to use those teeth on me, you would have done it by now," she pointed out. He blinked, clearly having no argument to counter that.

Instead, he looked back toward the rock and released her to go back to his pack. His motions were stiff as he scooped it up off the ground.

When he faced her, his jaw was no longer covering his teeth, but tension radiated from every inch of his burly frame.

Miranda stepped closer.

Then her foot caught on a root and she tripped forward. Govek lunged and caught her easily. His reflexes were insane.

"S-sorry." Her cheeks went red hot, more from how good it felt to have him catch her than of the embarrassment of tripping.

"Do you . . ."

"Do I?" she pressed.

"Do you want me to carry you?" he offered rapidly, showing her generous flashes of his teeth. The sound of his voice was crisper, and she wanted him to rumble words at her until she was reduced to contented jelly.

"I do."

He hesitated briefly before shifting his grip down her back and under her knees, curling his body around her. Her breath caught in her throat as her heart thundered. Then he swooped her off her feet and lifted her. His massive warm hands slung her up, so she was resting in the crook of his elbow, and he tucked her forehead into his neck.

"Keep your head here," he ordered gruffly, before adjusting his cloak so his face was hidden from her prying eyes.

She sighed heavily, wondering if hiding had been his true reason for offering to carry her, but she obeyed.

CHAPTER

EIGHT

Govek's face and hands were tingling, his mind was mush, and he could not pull his eyes away from the woman's chest. The blasted cloak was peeping open in the front, giving him a glorious view of her plump, round cleavage, which bobbed with her every word, threatening to spill out of her breast covering. Fuck, it was too distracting. He should close the cloak for her and end the temptation, but he could not close it without putting her down.

And he certainly wasn't going to put her down.

"I don't think I've ever been carried around like this. I've never really had a boyfriend. N-not that you're my boyfriend or whatever, I just mean like . . . I haven't been around many people buff enough to lift me."

Her easy babble helped to loosen the tension in his gut and, as her words flowed, her body gave into his arms, warm and supple and thoroughly distracting.

"So, thanks for carrying me," Miranda said. "I know I must be heavy."

He scoffed. "You weigh less than a rucksack of chicken bones."

"I probably look like one, too."

"You do not." Her frame would bulk up soon enough and hardly mattered in the list of her many attributes. Fades only knew how high his attraction would swell once she was clean. How much stronger the imprint would thrum.

Fuck, this was unsettling. Yerina's imprint had *never* gone so deep, even after three full seasons of bringing her boons and winning her favor.

He'd only given Miranda a few measly fish and the cloak.

It wasn't enough.

"Where are we going?" Miranda asked.

Not to war, that much was certain. His plans to join Karthoc were dashed completely.

But these woods were perilous too, and the only clan near was the one he'd just forsaken.

"Are you . . . taking me to where you live?"

Govek worked up the courage to push his cloak down and take in her sweet features. She didn't even flinch when she looked at him, even though his jaw was still lowered. Her eyes were bright and round with thick lashes. She worried her plump bottom lip with her teeth.

She was his. He knew not what they would do or where he would take her, but he would manage something.

"Govek?"

"I am taking you to a deeper part of the spring," he said, his voice lower and more abrupt than he intended. "To wash."

She shivered, and he tensed, certain she had finally recovered her senses. That the idea of bathing in his presence had popped the bubble of security and her fear of him would begin in full measure.

A brush at his chin forced the air from his lungs. Her warm fingers smoothed up the side of his face to the hinge of his jaw. "You don't have to hide, Govek. I'm fine."

He hadn't realized he'd concealed his teeth. "Hiding them is a courtesy to you."

"Courtesy?" Miranda's brow furrowed, and he nearly huffed with amusement.

"Yes. In my clan, we often keep our fangs hidden so that the humans do not become fearful." This was especially true during their regular trade with Oakwall Village, but most of the orcs in Rove Wood kept their fangs hidden as a show of respect. Govek had taken great pains to cover his even though it took more effort to conceal his much larger teeth. He had always hoped that the show of control may call his brethren to treat him with less suspicion and disquiet.

To think he'd spent so many seasons in discomfort only to have them throw him away.

"I mean, that ship has sailed, hasn't it? I already know what you look like now. And honestly, Govek, you look much better with your jaw in the right spot."

He searched her face for the barest hint of fear and found none. She was being earnest.

Fades help him. He lowered his jaw into its natural position, and she gifted him with the most dazzling smile he'd ever seen.

Then she shivered again. "You're really going to have me wash out here? It's going to be freezing."

"My skills with magic are not so wretched that I cannot fathom up a decent temperature for you."

She blinked up at him. Fuck, she was too pretty, and he needed to look away so she didn't see something in his face he was not ready to reveal.

"So, you can change water temperature with your magic? What else can you do?"

He hesitated, gut clenching. He should not have brought this up. The magic he held was unnatural. It was unsettling to all in this world.

But . . . not to Miranda. She was not of this world.

"Govek?" He savored the sound of his name on her lips, rolling the tender tone around in his mind until it filled him up.

"I only have the most basic magical skills," Govek said. He'd never received proper training. Hoping without regular communions, his magic would dwindle to nothing.

It hadn't worked, much to his father's chagrin.

"I have done well by you, my son, and worked tirelessly. Your rearing was trying, but I have ever stood at your side as support. I do so in this too. Your strength *will aid in your journey to Estwill, and I have every confidence that you will return a success."*

His gut twisted and his teeth clenched hard at the bitter memory of his father's words.

"That's okay." Miranda's voice was like a bell, a gentle chime that brought him back to the present. "I can't do any magic, so whatever you can do is better than me."

Of course not. She was human.

"I've never even seen magic before. Not real magic anyway."

"Your . . . *Earth* . . . does not have magic?"

Her gaze shot to his, haunted, glistening. He gritted his teeth. Remembering her words.

"They're all dead."

It was on the tip of his tongue to apologize for bringing up her painful past when she wrapped her slender arms about his neck and pressed herself more firmly into his embrace.

Fuck, he was lost. So abysmally lost. He cradled her to him and soaked up every drop of tenderness she was willing to give.

Soon she would realize what he was and spurn him. He'd learned that lesson well from Yerina. It was inevitable. But until that moment, he would relish every touch she graced him with.

"Tell me about magic." Her hot breath fanned over his nape and he barely stifled a shudder as bliss rolled through his gut.

Govek had spent so little of his life talking, had spent far too much of it alone either hunting in the woods or working on projects in his home, but if that is what his female needed to be content, he would do it.

He stuck to the basics, curating a balance that might quell her curiosity and stave off questions that were too prying. He did not want to lie to her, even if it meant keeping her from being frightened of him.

"Magic is a gift from the Fades. It helps us maintain our world while they are lost to slumber. It is mainly used to commune and conjure the seasons to flow properly."

"Commune and conjure?"

"Communing is the act of connecting to the Fades' power. Conjuring is the act of bending that power to one's will."

"So, you have to commune first and then you can conjure?"

"Yes, communing allows us to communicate with the Fades first and read what needs to be done to keep Faeda hale. Conjuring is not always required to enact their will." All orcs could commune, but only those born under the Rove Tree could conjure.

Blessed or cursed. His own communions and conjuring's often sparked without his conscious will. Instead of through calm and quiet like the rest of his brethren, it was his *anger* that struck up a connection to the Fades. And that anger burst forth magic so dangerous it could fell whole trees in a single blow, crack open massive chasms that could swallow entire homes, destroy entire cliffsides and cause devastating landslides.

His youth had been wrought with his blunders.

"It's really beautiful." Her words drew him out of his turmoil, and he looked down into her face. The red leaves fluttered down as the breeze caught them. Her complexion was dappled with sunlight from the canopy above. "We didn't have anything like this." Her lips trembled. "Orcs take care of the planet?"

"Orcs are tasked with the care of Faeda's surface. We bring balance to plant and animal life, ensuring that predators do not outmatch prey, that prey do not consume too much vegetation, and that plants maintain their order and grow steadily."

"How do you do that?"

"We have some control over weather, but our most vital act is to carry out the tasks communed to us."

It was not enough. Although the orcs of Rove Wood communed often, he hadn't seen any of Karthoc's warriors attempt to commune even once during their travels to Clairton. Which meant any tasks that the Fades were calling to be done outside of Rove were not heard.

"You can control the weather?" Miranda asked, tone bright with interest.

"I cannot." His voice was low. "But some of my brethren can cast rain in the morning and it would flood the land by the afternoon."

Tavggol had been gifted this way. His abilities were unmatched by any in Rove Wood Clan. His death had brought far more than sorrow.

Miranda soothed the tips of her fingers over the knuckles of the hand he had clasped around her knees. He found that his claws were extended.

"I apologize." Shame flattened him, and he moved to set her down.

"Nope." She clung to his neck again, squeezing him tight. "Don't you dare."

He huffed in surprise, but he didn't want to put her down either, so he readjusted her carefully, making certain his claws were well away from her flesh. "I have little control, Miranda. I am a danger to you."

Her snort of laughter flummoxed him. "If you knew the danger I'd just been through . . . you are by far the least of my troubles, Govek."

He wanted to question her, but the dread he'd seen in her face when the subject had been touched before was more painful than his own curiosity.

"So, is *your* primary job keeping the predator population under control?"

Govek tipped his head.

She quirked a smile, and the tension in his chest ebbed.

"You took down that wild cat pretty quick. I kinda assumed you'd honed that skill, or are you just naturally talented?"

Govek looked away. Karthoc had also been impressed with the veracity of Govek's attacks, but that was because his unhinged, magic-laced, battle craze had won them the day in Clairton without casualties.

"I am . . . *was* the hunter for my clan."

"You were the *only* hunter?" Miranda asked, scratching at the back of his neck. He held his breath, afraid even the slightest change might scare her off.

"Yes." There were many members of the clan who were skilled fisherman and a few who could trap small animals, but Govek was the only member who hunted for large game.

"And then you left to fight in the war?"

The bubble of contentment that her little scratches caused popped around him, and he straightened, gritting his teeth.

They'd sent him to his fucking *death*, and it was doubtful they would ever feel a moment of regret over it.

"Govek?" Miranda said quietly, but this time, her sweet voice and careful words did nothing to quell his anger.

THE SPRING'S current was slow in the area Govek had chosen, relatively deep, with sandy banks and large round boulders jutting out to form a lazy pool.

There was a natural rock wall at the far side where only a trickle drained through. He could heat this pool and the temperature would remain long enough for Miranda to bathe.

He set Miranda down in the sand. Water lapped against the golden banks and glittered in the daylight, reflecting the reds and yellows of the dying leaves that floated down with the breeze and sent lazy ripples through the water as they landed on the surface.

He was rarely one for sentiment, but even he could admit this place helped him to forget his troubles.

He swung off the pack and found some dried meat and bread. "Here."

"Thank you," she said, and ate without hesitation. He went to the edge of the water and kneeled. "What are you doing?"

"I'm going to heat the water for you." He hoped he could channel his anger properly so he could accomplish it.

"With magic?"

"Yes." His voice was strained.

Her steps drew near. "Can I watch?"

He tensed with uncertainty. He actively avoided conjuring magic as much as possible and had never had anyone request to watch him perform it.

But Miranda's eyes were bright, and her smile was soothing, and he could not deny her either the comfort of warm water or the act of watching him create it for her.

"You will not see much. Humans cannot see magic."

"And you can?" When he nodded, she quickly followed up. "What does it look like? In the movies it was always super sparkly and colorful. Is it similar?"

"It looks like waves of heat," he replied, puzzling over what a movie was.

Miranda kneeled next to him then, craning to see where his hands were dipped into the water. Her neck extended and the driving urge to bury his face into it and breathe in her scent spiked right through his guts.

The pungent odor of that vile tincture she was coated in barely stopped him. The pain might be worth it.

His control was in tatters.

Fuck. He rubbed a hand over his face, yanked his hair, and fought for reason.

"Are you okay?" Miranda asked, only making his wretched need for her worse. Why did she have to be so blasted *kind*?

"I'm fine," he snapped. "It just takes concentration."

Miranda moved away, shoulders slumped. "Sorry. I'll step over here and keep quiet."

The sight made his fists bunch. "You don't have to." He broke off with a heavy sigh and admitted, "The difficulty of it has nothing to do with you."

"You don't have to heat the water for me. I can take a sponge bath instead," she said. "You've done enough for me already."

The idea of her shivering on the bank while trying to wash was maddening. "You are my conquest. It is my honor to serve and protect you."

She gave a half smile and returned to her food. He flexed his hands in the water and centered his mind. Formed his thoughts around the anger that seemed ever present in his gut. It bloomed slowly as he focused on it, gingerly coaxing it to heed his will. He had to be *careful*.

He could not lose control and risk Miranda being hurt.

The swirling essence of Fade magic and might tingled up his spine and light flooded into his head. It was a pinprick now. Far below him. Almost too far for him to even grasp.

He'd never attempted to purposefully commune or conjure magic outside of Rove Wood before. The few times it had happened accidentally his power had been churned up by intense rage and grief.

The grief of finding his brother tortured to death.

His stomach felt like a pit, not just of sorrow, but of regret. He had committed many vile deeds throughout his life due to his inability to keep his anger in check and his magic under his control. But his actions that day, after discovering Tavggols body, had been a whole other kind of horror. The atrocity he'd committed at Clairton would always haunt him.

Gritting his teeth, Govek turned back to the task at hand, using the lingering pain from that wretched day to pull forth his connection to the Fades and bring about the conjuring of his magic. Wishing once again that he could be like his brethren. That he could pull his magic from feelings of serenity and calm. They made the act seem so dignified and peaceful.

Instead, he was forced to grow his fury and grief until it felt like a tight, red hot fist churning up his chest and stomach. He had to push it much higher and hotter than usual before the light from the Fades began to brighten in his mind. He knew this was because of his current location. Being deep in the outer woods with little to no connection to the Great Rove Tree and its blessings made communicating with the Fades difficult. Almost impossible.

It was no wonder that Karthoc's warriors and the other clans outside Rove Wood had given up trying to commune with them.

"So . . . what is a conquest again?" Miranda's voice was distant, and he tensed, reminding himself that his *mind* was far from her, not his physical body. Her light tone helped confirm that she was well, which made it much easier to draw in the Fades' light.

He found it difficult to form words but managed, "Conquests are human females."

"Human women who are cared for and protected by sentinels?"

"Yes." The light of the Fades was growing in a deep well of black within his mind's eye. Like a pool of dark water with a candle flickering at the bottom. He worked his way toward that light, using the tight ball of anger in his stomach to guide him. To drag him downward into it.

"But what do sentinels get out of the deal? Do you just enjoy the companionship? Do they stay with you long term?" Her voice sounded like it was underwater, garbled and thick. It took him a moment to process her words.

"Most human women return to their homes when their duty is complete," he finally replied. He could feel the light heating his skin now. Tingling up his fingers and swirling in his veins.

"Their duty?"

He was far too distracted when he elaborated. "Conquests bear the sons of sentinels."

Her sharp intake of breath cut through his concentration and his stomach dropped.

Govek yanked out of the communion and returned to full awareness. His eyes snapped open to assess his conquest's condition and found her unharmed, but thunderstruck.

Miranda had paled. Her emotions flickered across her face so quickly he couldn't keep track before she scowled and sputtered. *"Excuse me?"*

He could not think of words to combat her anger before she snapped, her voice loud and bold like thunder. "What the heck? I'm not having babies with you. You're a complete stranger. Is that why you helped me? So, you could convince me to have your kids?"

Govek was struck by the accusation. "That is *not* why I helped you, woman."

"Then why do you keep calling me this *conquest* thing? Do conquests have another purpose or something?"

"No . . . they don't." Why *had* he called her his conquest? Outside of wanting to protect her, she did not fit the role of one. Conquests only bore the sons of sentinels. There did not need to be emotional attachments involved, and sentinels certainly wouldn't be *imprinted* on their conquests.

And there was no doubt he was imprinted on her.

Nothing about this situation was predictable, but one thing he knew, he wasn't worthy of having children. His anger was too violent. His rage was uncontrolled.

And what if they were born like him? An abomination of the Fades, built like a warrior but able to conjure? Full of rage that tainted their magic?

Would his sons be subjected to the same isolation he was forced to endure?

"God*damn*, my planet explodes and now *this*?"

He blinked, looking up. Her world *exploded*?

"So, what? Your own women aren't good enough for you? Or is it the other way around?" She waved her hand up and down as her eyes raked over him.

Her words stung harder than he cared to admit. Building pain at the back of his throat and making his jaw come up around his teeth, as if hiding them would make him more human. More appealing to her. "There are no sentinel women."

"What?" Her voice rose. "How does that make sense?"

"It is by the Fades design."

"You mean your gods?" she asked, clearly incredulous.

"Yes." He did not know how to react to her disbelief. Her Earth did not have Fades?

"You're telling me you guys can get human women pregnant? There's no way that's possible." Irritation flashed behind his eyes, but she kept on. "You're not even human and you're saying your DNA is supposed to just miraculously match up with mine? That's crazy. I mean, *look* at you."

Govek's irritation quickly flipped to anger, and his muscles clenched, trembling. He knew not what this "DNA" was, but the insult was clear enough. And the implication that they were not compatible hurt much more than he wanted to admit.

"You're built like a freaking Greek god and I'm a third your size. How could I, or *any* human, possibly carry a baby that *big*?"

Govek's anger faded slightly, and he gathered his sanity. Fuck, he could *not* lose control like this. Not with her. He had to calm. *Calm.*

He watched the unflinching woman tap her chin as she examined him with a furrowed brow. Her unabashed curiosity and unflinching courage helped soothe him further.

"How big are your babies exactly?"

Govek blinked rapidly, unsure how to respond to the question. He'd never held a newborn before, was not even allowed near the orc sons, so he could barely venture a guess.

"Sorry, I'm getting off topic," she waved as if trying to smack the subject right out of the air. "Seriously, though, are you honestly saying there are no orc women? I've never heard of a species that didn't have its own female population before. That required a *different* species to procreate."

"There are no orc women—or goblin women, or sylph women," Govek confirmed slowly, confusion radiating down into his chest to smother out the last smoldering remains of his anger.

"So, there were *never* sentinel women?"

"No."

Her lips parted, eyes widened, flickering in thought. Something was going on inside her mind and Govek would have given his right leg to know what it was.

"So . . . orcs *want* to have babies with humans. Like . . . I mean . . ."

He tipped his head. "You mean . . ."

"I mean, you find me *attractive* enough to have babies with me?"

Govek *never* expected that to be her next question. He was so taken aback that he couldn't find words to answer her.

But Miranda had no such issue. She rushed on. "I mean, objectively, of course. Like you could be convinced to find me, er—or I mean, you could find *any* woman appealing enough to . . . you know. I don't mean me specifically, not at all, just *anyone.* Any human woman. Or—"

"Miranda." His heart thundered in his ears.

"Y-yes?"

"What is a Greek god?"

"A what?" Her brow furrowed in confusion, and then realization flooded her face. Her cheeks went bright pink as she bowed her head. "Oh, uh. Well, you know—"

"I don't," he said low and slow. "That is why I am asking."

"Oh god." Her words were so quiet he doubted she intended for him to hear them. "Don't talk like that. It's too much."

Understandably, she didn't realize how good orc hearing was—especially when it came to the female an orc was imprinted on. His chest tightened, knowing his growling must be unsettling her.

And then the scent of her arousal flooded his senses. Sweet and rich, like honey warmed from the sunlight.

Fuck, he almost didn't believe his own senses. Almost wondered if this was a delusion. But another deep inhale proved it.

She wanted him.

How was that even *possible*?

Govek gulped hard. Fire burning in his gut, confusion churning. "Miranda?"

"It's, uh, well, you know what gods look like, right?" She fidgeted.

"The Fades appear as light."

"Oh." She pressed her hands to her cheeks, large eyes looking up into his. "That's not it then."

"Miranda," Govek said low, watching a shiver course over the woman's frame. Fuck, her scent was growing so heady and thick he could almost taste it.

He wasn't even certain what he'd done to earn this. The

food he'd gifted her was almost insulting compared to what Yerina had demanded.

"A Greek god is like . . . the epitome of beauty, like the highest rank of hunk. Ten out of ten hottie."

Blast. He didn't understand half the words she said, but her meaning was clear enough. He raked a hand through his hair.

Govek was no fool. He knew what he looked like. Was she bolstering his ego because she was still worried he may abandon her in these woods?

Miranda's face had turned a bright red, and she began to babble delightfully. "I mean, not necessarily that . . . that *all* orcs are attractive. I don't know cause I haven't met all of them, but at least with you it's—oh jeez. You gotta stop me before I get going like this or I'll say things I regret."

He certainly didn't regret anything she'd said so far. He wanted her to talk more. Lay her every thought out for him to examine.

"What do other orcs look like? Do they all look like you?"

Govek's gut pitched. "No. They do not."

He did not fit the aesthetic of Rove Wood orcs in any way. They were slender, unblemished, and regal. He was a beast next to them.

He stuck out among the warrior orcs too, even with all their brawn and strength. Like a dirt clod among smooth river rocks. At least the warriors were well proportioned. At least their hands were not so massive, a trait necessary to wield magic properly. At least their muscles were not so accentuated and bulging.

Govek did not fit in anywhere. He had no place.

"I wonder what a female orc would look like."

The comment snapped him out of his thoughts and his brow furrowed, nose curled. "I cannot imagine female orcs being very pleasing to the eye."

A giggle sounded, but Miranda covered her mouth with her hands, concealing the expression and disappointment made his chest tight. "Sorry. I'm sorry. I don't mean to laugh." His brows rose, and she admitted, "I was kinda trying to imagine a female version of you."

He snorted. "Fuck, that must have been a horror."

She giggled again, the sound breaking through her fingers and flooding through him. "You're pretty manly, or should I say orcly? What's proper?"

"The fuck if I know."

"I think manly works. Regardless, I can't picture it. Honestly, you seem pretty human to me."

He blinked, reeling from her admission. "I'm unsure how you have overlooked the significant physical differences."

Her hand lowered and the sight of her gorgeous smile forced air from his lungs, causing him to lose his breath. "I guess that's true."

Hoping to broaden that smile into a beam, he said, "Perhaps it would help if I wore a gown."

"I—*what*?"

"Then you could see what a female orc might look like."

His efforts were rewarded instantly as Miranda burst with full, rich laughter. The sound was so sweet and alluring that his jaw loosened, and he did not even bother to shut it.

"Oh my god, Govek." She wiped at her eyes, her smile still beaming bright.

This was, perhaps, the first time he had ever pulled a woman into mirth. Warmth burst in his chest and soaked through his veins, breathed life right into him. She was so beautiful in her happiness it was almost painful.

"I don't think even a dress would work, though." Miranda's tone was light and her eyes danced. "You're definitely an orc. A really badass orc."

His brows furrowed. She didn't appear angry but her words sounded like an insult. What had he done to earn her ire? What could he gift her to make that ire quell?

She rushed in, "I mean, cool—er, awesome, sexy—ah frick. I'mma shut up now."

Govek's throat tightened. Was Miranda upset with him or was she complimenting him?

"Go ahead and do your thing," she insisted. "I swear I won't bother you. Again."

He wished she would. He wished she would make easy demands of him the way Yerina had. Tell him *exactly* what she wanted so he could get on with earning her favor.

But he supposed the bath was what she truly desired.

With a nod to her, he turned back to the spring and dipped his hands into the icy water again, connecting to the Fades' energy and forcing his way through the grime of the outer woods.

The light went from a pinprick to blazing inferno so fast it blinded him.

Govek yelped in shock and rocketed back from the water. His head swam from the magical surge he'd lost control of. Fuck, it hadn't even been his temper that had made the magic spiral. His muscles tingled, and he flexed his hands, cutting off his connection to the Fades completely.

"Are you okay?" Miranda was near him now, crouching

at his side. Her gaze was on his hands. "Are your hands okay? Oh god. That water is *boiling*."

Boiling? He looked to find the pool bellowing steam and bubbling. It put off enough heat that he felt it from where he sat on the bank.

What the fuck had happened? He'd never been able to connect to the Fades so quickly. Not even at Clairton. Not even from within the Great Rove Tree itself.

"Are your hands burned?" Gentle touches brushed his skin. The spring's healing properties had already taken the burns from blisters to simply raw. But he certainly wasn't about to stop Miranda's gentle, caressing touches. And fuck all, did she touch him! Her gentle fingertips grazed over each line of his palms, traced up his fingers, soothed over the tips where his claws were hidden. She trailed her hands up his wrists and over his forearms, and Govek resisted the need to shiver.

Fades be praised! Her touch was bliss.

"I think you're okay," she said, her voice as much a balm as the spring water.

"Don't go in yet," he ordered. "It's too hot."

She shot him a harsh, exasperated look and he stilled, mesmerized. Not even Yerina had been brave enough to look at him this way. "You really think I'm that dumb?"

"No." The word came out strangled.

She reached up and rustled his hair. Judging from the smirk, she intended to be playful, but fuck, it felt so blasted good. His eyes fluttered closed and he let out a sigh so gusty it emptied his lungs.

"You're a little touch starved, aren't you?"

Govek's eyes shot open, and he confirmed that she looked just as breathless as her tone had portrayed. Her cheeks were pink, her full lips were red, and her eyes sparkled in the dazzling sunlight.

He wanted to keep her.

He wanted her to *want* him. Not as a conquest, but as a *mate.*

Fades, where had that even *come* from? He was losing his blasted head. He knew that. But he still wanted every drop of Miranda's affection. He wanted to be greedy with it. Keep it all for himself. He wanted her to cleave to him and want him and grow her own attachment to him; to mirror the imprint that was raging through his veins, ravaging his senses.

He would gift her any number of boons to make that happen, perform any acts and go to whatever ends her whims demanded.

His mind drifted back to the one thing she clearly *didn't* desire.

"I swear to you, Miranda," Govek said. "I have no intention of treating you as a conquest and having you bear my son."

She blinked and sat back slightly. "You don't . . . want to have a child with me?"

"I do not."

Miranda's face paled, and her expression slacked.

"I leave you to prepare for your bath." With that, he got to his feet, turned his back, and moved to the tree line to give her some privacy.

Only to freeze in place as Miranda yelled, "Why the heck *not*?"

MIRANDA

W *hat the flip did I just say?*

Miranda fidgeted and chewed her lips. She should be *happy* he didn't want to force her to have his baby. He was a stranger, for god's sake.

But she wasn't happy. She wasn't happy at all.

"I mean . . . I mean . . ." she faltered as Govek slowly turned to stare her down. His eyes were way too expressive, and she would rather bury herself alive than meet them. "Is there something about me that makes you think I wouldn't be a good mom?"

He blinked slowly, looking incredulous. "Your ability as a mother holds no bearing."

"My ability to be a good mother holds no bearing on my ability to be a mother? That makes absolutely no sense, Govek."

"Conquests do not raise orc babes."

"They . . . don't? So, they're just surrogates or something?"

He sighed, crossing his arms. "I know not what a surrogate is. Conquests agree to carry the son to term in exchange for boons. Often, they return to their homes to carry out the pregnancy and return the babe after they are born."

She'd been all geared up to ramble on about her experience with kids, but his response knocked her flat. She knew surrogacy had been very common on Earth, but she couldn't imagine handing her tiny baby over to anyone.

"I don't want to be a conquest. I want to raise my babies. I want to be a mom."

Govek's complexion drained, and his brows shot up and Miranda suddenly realized what she'd just said.

"I mean, not right now, of course. And not necessarily with you. Not that I *wouldn't* have kids with you if we ended up—er. I'm just not ready to have kids, Govek. With anyone." God, she'd just survived the *apocalypse*. "But I'm not writing it off entirely either. If things eventually, one day, end up going that direction, I would be down for babies with you."

Oh frick, that was *not* better. Miranda wished she could yank out her own tongue and slap it, but now Govek looked like his head was screwed on too tight and she rushed on. "I only say that because . . . because I want to know why you *wouldn't* ever want to have kids with me. You've only known me for a day, and you've made up your mind already, so there must be *something* about me that forced that conclusion. I just want to know what it is so I can fix it."

That was a little better, right? She'd saved herself?

Miranda looked around at the sandy ground, wondering how hard it would be to bury herself in it.

"You would be 'down' for babies?" She looked back up into Govek's green-gold eyes. His brows were pinched in confusion. "With *me*?"

She gulped and fidgeted. "I mean, why *not*?"

There was a stretch of silence that ate her alive before Govek responded coldly.

"I do not intend to take you as a true conquest because *I* would not make a good father."

Miranda's spine straightened. "What? Why do you think that?"

"I do not think it. I *know*." His voice was low, harsh. It lashed with its certainty and left her feeling stung.

His expression was too familiar. She'd seen it many, *many* times in the faces of the other kids she'd grown up with, but still she asked, "How do you know?"

He shot her a dark look, and it had all the information she needed. She'd been raised in a group home, for god's sake. Kids didn't end up in group homes because they had decent families and home lives.

And for every person like Miranda, who wanted to adopt a kid in need because of their own shitty childhood, there was another who *didn't* want to have children for the exact same reason.

She was about to say something. She'd been to enough counselors and therapists to know the right words. But just as she opened her mouth, she heard a cry, a striking wail, in the distance.

A horror she never thought she'd be subjected to again.

An air-raid siren.

She froze solid, ears straining, gut twisting. Her

forehead broke out in a sweat, and her heart pounded in her chest until the rapid thrum made it difficult to breathe.

They had no bombs here. Surely, they didn't. So, there wouldn't be a need for a siren, right?

Right. She was imagining it. Her stupid anxiety was getting the best of her. She was just too keyed up after everything that had happened. It was fine. Everything was okay. It's okay. It's—

"Miranda."

She jerked, meeting Govek's emerald green eyes.

"We're safe here, right?"

His forehead creased, but he assured her. "Yes, I smell no predators near."

She wanted to press for more information. Ask about the war. About what kind of technology they used to fight. But she was too much of a coward to get the words out.

"Take your bath, Miranda. Before the water goes cold."

A bath. Right. A bath in a spring in the middle of the woods. Any civilization too primitive to have hotels certainly wouldn't have nuclear bombs.

She shook off the fear and set on another task. Deciding what clothes to take off. The cloak and shoes were a no-brainer, but all she would have after taking those off was the gym shorts, granny panties, and the sports bra, all of which desperately needed washing.

Miranda took off her shoes, cloak, and shorts. What remained was enough to be considered a bathing suit.

Her eyes trained to where Govek stood with his back to her at the edge of the tree line. "You don't have to stand there. You can face me."

He choked. "What?"

She tried to hide her smile. "I'm not naked, and I'd rather be able to chat with you while I'm bathing."

She could see the line of his shoulders tense at her words, but he turned anyway. The pilfered underwear was nowhere near attractive or revealing. But now, with Govek's hot gaze darkening because of her silhouette, she was starting to like them. His eyes looked golden in the dappled light, glowing as they speared through her.

He hadn't seen her without the cloak since he'd been a step away from death. Why hadn't she remembered that?

Her lips parted, and she focused on his unclenched hands. They twitched toward her, as if he might be thinking about pulling her into his embrace.

Or, if she was lucky, maybe bending her over the nearest boulder.

She bit her tongue, determined to hear what he had to say first.

"Woman, was there something you wanted?"

What the frick?

"Uh, I mean . . ." Miranda fidgeted, thrown off completely. Hadn't he been checking her out? Now she felt stupid.

His brows twitched. "Miranda, I am willing to go to whatever lengths to please you. You only need to tell me what you desire."

Her whole body went hot.

Hoo boy! He was flirting now, right? Or was that just her own wishful thinking? She had the *worst* flirting skills. She'd never had time or money for much more than the occasional video date. All of which had ended in utter disappointment.

"What are you offering?" Miranda asked, a little desperate.

Govek hesitated, and his throat worked. "I could attempt to hunt for you. If I am lucky, I could find a hare."

Her excitement dwindled. "A hare? Like a rabbit?"

"Yes."

"For . . . a pet?"

Govek blinked, momentarily flustered, and Miranda forced a hand over her mouth to stop from laughing. "You want to keep it as a *companion*?"

"Dude, I don't know. You're the one offering me weird shit." Miranda's voice was a little too shrill. "Look, I don't need anything, all right? I'm perfectly fine with what I've got. Even though it's basically nothing." She managed some bravery and gestured at her makeshift bikini, drawing his attention down her body.

His eyes raked over her and Miranda held her breath, waiting for him to *finally* make a comment.

He didn't make a sound, didn't even blink.

His non-response had her body breaking out with goosebumps from the overwhelming embarrassment. Desperate to distract from it, her stupid mouth blurted, "I stole these."

"You *stole* your undergarments?" His eyes shot to her face with his nose wrinkled in either shock or disgust. She couldn't decide which was worse.

Hysterical laughter born from sheer panic bubbled up her throat and she bit her cheek to stop it.

But she couldn't stop her horrific penchant for speaking when she should remain silent. "I mean, I guess. Technically, the person who owned them was dead before I took them."

Govek blinked slowly, eyes bulging.

Goddamn. There was no recovering from this.

With that in mind, she hurried into the water. It was deliciously warm, but that barely did anything to quell her tense muscles and only added heat to her embarrassment.

She considered dunking her head as well. Maybe if she stayed down long enough, Govek would forget she'd ever opened her mouth.

Maybe she'd drown and just end it already.

"Should I be worried about you robbing me of my clothes?"

His voice was low with mirth. She chanced a glance over her shoulder and found him smirking. She swallowed. "Depends. Do you have a hoodie?"

He clearly didn't know what a hoodie was. "I only have what I'm currently wearing and perhaps an extra shirt. You are welcome to them if you wish."

She snorted, carefully sitting down. The sandy bottom was soft, and the warm water lapped at her chin. Her embarrassment eased. "So, what? I rob you blind and leave you naked?"

"If you want. Then we would match."

"Excuse me. I have panties and a top on," she countered.

"Panties and a top that leave nothing to the imagination," Govek said thickly. He leaned against a nearby boulder. The very one she wanted him to bend her over.

She was already in this far. Miranda reached down and slipped off her underwear, giving them a good scrub before lifting them out. "You know what? Catch!"

Her aim was wretched, but Govek handled it like a

champ, lurching forward a few paces. Her panties splat into his hand, revealing what they were in an instant.

To his credit, he didn't drop them. "What the fuck?"

"What? You said it left nothing to the imagination. Might as well take them off." She took advantage of his distracted state and started scrubbing her body. The soft sand did wonders to exfoliate away the grime, but she still wished she had soap.

"You're a madwoman," Govek muttered, and she noticed he'd slung her panties into a patch of sun on one of the rocks.

"You must like it, or you would have left me already," she grinned. "Or maybe you haven't noticed until now?"

"I've been well aware." He kept his eyes averted. "I began questioning your sanity the moment you mentioned you liked to sit on babies."

"Sit on—? What?" It took a moment for her to realize what he meant. "Oh god! You mean babysitting? Is that why you thought I wouldn't be a good mom? Because you think I sit on babies?"

"No."

His quick dismissal forced a laugh out of her. "So, you'd have kids with me if I sat on babies for fun?"

He scowled. "Just tell me what babysitting is, Miranda."

Still chuckling, she managed, "It's watching kids for parents. They pay me to mind them while they're busy."

He paused for a moment, considering, before finally saying, "That has nothing to do with sitting."

The flat retort hit her hard and laughter burst out of her chest. Her eyes watered. "Govek, stop it or I am going to drown!"

"Be careful with your jests, woman, or I might just

attempt to rescue you and then you truly wouldn't have anything left to the imagination." His voice was lighter now, easier. But any trace of the smile he might have had was gone before she could wipe the blur of tears from her eyes.

Disappointed, she decided to push further.

"Not quite," she said, ducking her shoulders down below the water's surface to take off the sports bra before throwing it his direction. He caught it easily. "There, now nothing is left."

For some reason, she'd expected nothing more from him than another quick retort and more eye aversion. Instead, Govek froze with the sports bra in his hand, eyes fixed on the water where her chest was submerged. She saw his throat work in a gulp.

She'd forgotten about the fishing from the night before.

He could easily see under the water despite the ripples.

Warmth flooded her stomach, and she found herself tempted to squirm. To push her breasts up. To attract him further.

Something was wrong with her, but she didn't care because it felt too damn good.

"You're shameless." His voice was strangled as he tossed her bra to sit on the rock next to the panties.

"Tell me you don't like it and I'll stop," she said, giving him, and possibly herself, one last out before they were both in too deep.

But Govek shot his smoldering gaze down her body again, licking delicious pleasure up her spine. "You better not stop."

Hoo boy! She was in trouble.

"Get to washing or we're going to have to make camp here," Govek muttered, still not looking away. Miranda hesitated, stomach fluttering with mixed emotions as she continued to wash. The intensity of his eyes was hotter than the water, but his posture was rigid. Arms crossed, back straight.

The slight bulge in his pants betrayed him.

"So, I'm not doing any of the usual conquest things," she said a little breathlessly. It was an odd sensation, to be both embarrassed and excited. "What *am* I doing?"

"Anything you want."

Her cheeks hurt from smiling. She carefully scrubbed her arms, moving up toward her chest. "Hmm, you sure you wanna give me that kind of power? My imagination is pretty crazy."

"I'll take the risk," he almost purred, gaze stuck to her hands as she bathed.

She shot him a mischievous grin that made his face pale. "In that case, I want my name tattooed on your ass."

His brows shot up, and he paused before saying, "Only if you do the tattooing."

"Y-you don't want me to do that," Miranda insisted, suddenly regretting her teasing. He sounded sincere. Would he really let her tattoo something on his butt? "I have *horrible* handwriting." He was so sculpted, a fricking wall of muscle. She tried to imagine what his naked ass might look like and heat pooled in her stomach.

"What better way to immortalize it, then?"

"It would flipping *hurt*," she laughed. He *had* to be joking, right? She could only imagine tattoo equipment in this era was pointed sticks and hammers.

"A permanent mark on my flesh *would* be quite a weighty boon, but I'm sure you'd find a way to make it up to me."

Her laugh died in her chest, and the heat in her belly turned into an inferno. Her thighs clenched, and she sank deeper into the spring until her mouth was covered by the water.

Was he sure he didn't want to make babies?

Did they have birth control here?

Still squirmy and raw, Miranda swam toward a rock jutting up from the surface near the center. "I'm, uh, going to wash my hair."

"Miranda."

She turned to find Govek standing near the edge of the pool, his posture tensed, his muscles bulging. His hair was disheveled and framing his face.

More heat rolled through Miranda's gut, made her squirm and ache. Worse than it had when he'd gotten all rumbly about the "Greek god" thing.

Damn. She wanted him.

Gulping hard, she managed past her own reservations and asked breathlessly, "Do you . . . want to help?"

His emerald eyes widened, glittering. A shudder raked over his shoulders.

And then he swung off his cloak.

Before she could even manage a full breath, Govek had turned to dig through his pack. He put on brown leather gloves, which confused her to no end, and retrieved a palm sized, corked vile, which was a mystery.

Then he wrenched off his shoes.

And his *pants.*

Her heart skittered to a blazing halt at the sight of his bare legs, the muscles of his calves. The shape of his thighs where they met the firm globe of his ass.

He was still wearing a stupid pair of black boxer-like underwear. She wanted to rip them off.

He turned to face her, and she got a glimpse of him head-on. Huge frame. Rippling abs. Strong jaw.

The tight-fitting shorts outlined the—now clear—bulge of his cock. Her breath left her in a rush.

She enjoyed big toys, but Govek was massive enough to put them to shame. Nervousness and excitement danced in her veins as he lifted his head slightly and scented the air. He growled low, stalking toward her, water splashing around him.

Oh, she was in *big* trouble and she couldn't wait.

"Turn around," Govek demanded when he was still ten or so feet away.

She resisted the urge to pout, eyes still stuck on his groin, which she now could hardly see because of the water's depth. "Why?"

He let out a low rumbling growl that forced her eyes back to his face. His expression was tense as he teetered the bottle before her eyes. "I am offering to fix your hair."

"Is that shampoo?"

"Shampoo?"

"Hair cleaner."

"In a way. It is a tincture. Magic."

She clicked her tongue in thought. "You make a magic hair tincture for humans?"

Why was she so disappointed it was only for her hair?

"It is technically for healing, but it will work just as well."

"Oh. You don't have to waste it on me."

"Turn around," Govek said.

She finally obeyed and a zing of excitement instantly

replaced all the disappointment when he put his gloved hands on her waist, forcing her to move backward, settling her between his legs with her back deliciously close to his chest.

Dang, having him on the bank watching her bathe was nothing compared to having him so close. Her skin prickled as she squirmed, resisting the urge to cover her bare breasts and cross her legs.

It didn't matter. He'd already seen it all.

So instead, she rested her hands on his knees and her elbows on his thighs. He sucked in a breath.

"Is this okay?" she asked a little more breathlessly than she had intended. "Do you want me to move?"

"*No*," he grated, making her shudder again as delight bloomed in her stomach.

Wet leather grazed her cheeks as he trailed his fingers over them, pulling her hair back. Goosebumps broke out on her neck.

"Tell me if I do something you find unpleasant."

Her chest tightened as he began to work the knots from her hair, cupping water to soak it, and smoothing it into compliance. He was so brutal, yet inexplicably capable of such gentleness. Every careful pass of his fingers through her strands had her leaning into his touch for more. He worked sighs out of her so easily it was like he'd done this a million times.

"You're . . . really good at this." She was in such bliss she'd let him get away with everything. Lord, she hoped he wanted to.

"Not that good," he muttered, frustration clear. "I may need to cut some."

"Go ahead."

"I will need to use my claws to do so."

"That's fine." Her skin tingled, imagining him raking those claws along her scalp and down her back. The inside of her thighs. He'd run the sharp edges against her sensitive flesh and sooth the tingling sting with the pad of his warm fingers.

Did he really only want to touch her hair? She couldn't find the bravery to ask as he took off a glove and began slicing away her tangles. It was painless and she could tell he hadn't needed to cut much, but she still wished she had a mirror.

"I want to use this boon now," Govek said, reaching around to show her the corked bottle. He'd already put the glove back on.

She'd barely nodded before the cool liquid was poured onto her head. It smelled strongly of lavender.

He soothed his hands into her hair, soaking her scalp with the oil, sending tingling pleasure through her. It skittered down her spine and lapped at her stomach. Pooled liquid heat between her legs.

"Lean back now," he ordered. She hesitated, keenly aware of how hard her nipples were, of how slick she was between her thighs. Would he notice any of that?

She closed her eyes, too nervous to look at him as he pressed her shoulders. Slowly, she sank down until she was floating on her back in the water. Breathless and trying not to move.

A harsh growl danced bliss through her limbs and her eyes burst open to find Govek's piercing gaze dancing over her body, skewering her through with heat and deep pleasure.

Heaven help her. Any sense that he only wanted to wash her hair was completely destroyed.

"Keep your eyes closed," he demanded roughly, grazing a gloved finger over them to force them shut.

"Why?"

He didn't answer, and she supposed she didn't really need one. She could guess it was for the same reason he hid his face while he was carrying her and kept getting confused by her compliments.

She couldn't blame him. She was self-conscious, too. It took every ounce of her willpower not to cross her legs and cover her breasts with her arms.

She shut her eyes to slits, so a little light remained. She was reluctant to be in complete darkness. The slight scratch of his claws under the gloves distracted her as he gently began to rub her scalp, fan out her hair around her head so he could get between the strands, and smooth out the oil.

This felt way too good. It burned need into every cell of her being.

He raked his fingertips across her overstimulated senses until she was desperate enough to lose some of her reservations. "*Govek.*"

He let out a harsh sound, pulling her up and pressing her back into the heat of his chest. He was even hotter than the water. His hard muscles twitched against her bare skin. His breath was jagged against her ear.

She shivered, pushing her hips back into his groin and felt the hard length of him jerk.

A moan broke from her lips.

Oh god. Was she *really* doing this?

"*Fuck*," he snarled, "Can . . ." He took a deep breath,

hands still clutching her shoulders. "I'll catch a hare for you to keep. So, can I touch you, Miranda?"

A nervous laugh left her. "I don't actually want a hare, Govek."

"What do you want then?"

She tensed a little. "I don't want anything." She felt him go rigid against her back. "I don't want anything but you, Govek. Just you."

He gulped. "So, I can touch you?"

She let out a long breath and all her tension and nervousness went with it.

"Yes, Govek. You can."

CHAPTER

TEN

GOVEK

S he said *yes*. He couldn't fucking believe it.

But the scent on her couldn't be denied, not even the water could dilute it. It was *incredible*. Raw and rich. Honey and passion. Like the Fades had dredged up his deepest fantasy and made it real.

Inexplicably, washing her hair with a simple tincture had been enough. She'd provided heady moans and squirmed against his cock while he raked her scalp. He shivered.

Govek's nerves sparked as he worked on his courage, his control. He forced his mind to calm so he could relish and memorize every moment of this gift.

Miranda's body was sheer perfection—rosy-tipped nipples and dark curls between her thighs. She needed more meat on her, more fat to soften her limbs, but he could accomplish that easily. He would relish the task.

But not nearly as much as he would enjoy this one.

He wrapped an arm around the smooth expanse of her stomach and pulled her into his torso, tucking her head into the crook of his neck so she couldn't easily see him. He could not risk her rejecting him midway through.

Like he'd been rejected before.

"Govek?" Her voice was caught between curiosity and pleading. She tried to turn, but he tightened his hold and she didn't fight further. "What are you doing?"

"Shut your eyes," he demanded, voice thick.

"Why?" She reached her hand back and her fingertips connected with the side of his face, working down his jaw. He barely withheld a hiss as jolts of pleasure skittered down his spine.

His thoughts frayed.

"Close them." He was strung so tight. If she refused him now, he would be shattered. Worse than he'd ever been.

She hummed. The unhappy sound tore at him, but the sight of her eyes fluttering closed gave him courage.

He grazed his hands down her shoulders, focusing on his need to be gentle, soothing his desire to take command, locking away his instincts.

Calm, he demanded of himself. The insistence was so difficult it made his muscles ache.

Miranda let out a little gasp as his fingers grazed over her collarbone and down to the swell of her pink-tipped breasts. They were perfect. Soft and lush. Dappled with beads of water. His hands were shaking as he paused, giving her a moment to deny him before he went lower.

Instead, she thrust her chest up, beckoning him. And when he stroked his fingers over the firm tips of her nipples, she expelled a gusty moan and relaxed against his shoulder.

The scent of her arousal burst in his nose, sweet and thick. Fuck, did the heights of her lust have an end?

Govek bit his tongue to keep from growling in pleasure.

Thrumming her nipples, he sent her body into rippling shivers, shuddering against his cock. The pleasure in him mounted, danced over his skin, and clenched hard in his gut.

Fuck, she was so *responsive*.

A louder groan fell from her lips and she reached up to grab one of his hands. For an abysmal moment, he was certain she would push him away.

Instead, she forced it *lower*, pushing it down toward her core.

"What are you doing?" His breath hitched, hardly believing she was already letting him touch her here, even as she spread her legs to make room for his hand.

"You don't want to?" she asked, though she didn't stop moving his fingers.

"I want to."

"Good." She pushed his fingers over the flat of her stomach and passed her belly button. Down between her folds.

"Oh!" She let out a strangled sound as he grazed gently over her most sensitive place. He couldn't feel much through the gloves, but he was experienced enough with this act to know where to touch and what reactions to watch for.

She opened her eyes.

He gritted his teeth, tension dimming his own arousal even as hers bloomed sweet in his nose, coated his throat. "Close them."

Fuck, he'd said it too harshly.

But instead of tensing and pushing away, Miranda's body relaxed, and her eyes went to half-mast. A groan left her lips. His fingers slicked, gliding more easily, telling him she must have grown wetter. Her nipple beaded under his thumb.

He gritted his teeth. He'd imagined that, right? It almost seemed as if she'd grown *aroused* from his growling.

Govek had no time to dwell on this knowledge, as Miranda's exquisite responses to his spearing fingers made his heart seize. She pushed against the back of his hand in a steady rhythm. Bucking and whimpering. Moving him how she wanted, using him.

Being used so selfishly had never felt so good. He twitched helplessly between her folds and it made her gasp. He swirled his fingers over her breast, and she dug her heals into the sand, kicking it up under the water.

Everything seemed to please her. Every touch heightened her. His head swam with it. Drunk on her pleasure, dizzy from disbelief.

Her grip eased, and she allowed him to explore freely. He slicked his finger high to circle around the top of her folds, where he knew she would be the most sensitive, and was rewarded with her thighs quivering.

"Oh, Govek that's . . . it's so *different*."

Different? Different from what?

Was she referring to him being an orc? His stomach churned. Her eyes were open again. If she tipped her head, she would see him.

"Lower. Like this," she said, pushing his hand down. She forced his palm to press hard into the top of her folds and separated his index and middle fingers.

Moved them to her entrance.

Govek resisted, muscles tensing, even as his cock twitched with want.

It was far too soon for that. She couldn't possibly be ready.

He wasn't either. He wasn't ready for this to be over.

Her resistance was puny, and he swirled his fingers up to graze through her folds again.

"Too much," she hissed.

He froze as the honeyed smell of her arousal dimmed. The water chilled the flames licking through his veins.

What had he done *wrong*? She'd been begging for this a moment ago.

"Lower," she demanded, eyes opening wider. She pushed him downward again, arching her neck.

He gritted his teeth, wishing he could feel more passed the leather gloves. "Eyes *closed*, Miranda."

She whimpered and hesitated.

"Closed," he almost begged.

"It's too dark," she said. The trembling in her voice cut him.

Too dark?

"I . . . don't want to be alone."

She didn't want to be *alone*? What the fuck did *that* mean? Was his hand on her not enough? Could she not feel his cock throbbing against her back? His guts twisted with indecision.

He couldn't let her see him. He *knew* it would ruin it, but he couldn't force her to do something that caused her distress, either.

Clenching his teeth, Govek grazed her nipple one last time, earning another bliss racked whimper, before moving his hand up to her chin, slipping his fingers around her cheek and ear to keep her head in place.

"Ooh," she whimpered as he tipped her head away from

him. She squirmed against his grip and brought her knees up.

Fuck, he couldn't have her fighting him in this. He adjusted his legs over hers, holding them in place and apart. She squirmed and wriggled.

The moment he had her pinned, the honeyed fragrance swelled to dizzying heights as her desire bloomed. It clouded every space of his mind. His instincts roared to life like never before.

Her legs jerked against him, sending erotic need blazing down his spine. He wanted to cage her like she was his prey, hold her down, tighten his grip until she couldn't even twitch.

Take her like the beast he was, hard and fast and *ruthless*.

His mind blazed, ripped apart at the conflict warring behind his eyes. He could not give into his urges. He would ruin this.

Miranda's gasps and moans were too sweet. Her fucking scent was *everywhere*. Thick and needy. He craved it, pushed for it. Dug fingers into her core again to force it higher. Her hips bucked as two digits skirted passed her entrance despite her hands pushing at him to enter.

"Why?" she whined, though he had no idea what she meant and any elaboration she might have given was cut off with a whimper as he swirled his fingers again. Lighter. Circling wide instead of flicking. "Oh, yes. That's good."

She was so blissfully transparent. So eager. He didn't have to rely on the scent of her arousal to know she was burning for him.

Govek buried his face in her neck and heaved another

gulp of her. His jaw threatened to unhinge. He was losing his fucking mind.

Somehow, she wriggled her heel out of his confines and dug into his calf, trying to break free of him so she could roll her hips into his hand.

Or escape.

Heat speared him. The dark urge to hunt her roared to life, and he barely quelled it.

He firmed his grip on her chin, warning her.

It worked. She froze, groaning, panting harshly. Shivers coursed down her limbs.

"Don't fight me." He tried to keep his voice smooth.

"But I want to."

Fades help him. He bit his tongue until it bled to keep from growling.

"Please, Govek."

Her pleading almost broke him. The pressure in his groin was agony. The tension of his tight underclothes against his oversensitive cock was maddening. In a blink, he was going to rip the fucking things off and truly lose himself in her.

"Govek," she groaned, squirming against him. Her voice was like syrup, sweet and dangerous as it swept into every crevice of his mind.

Her head dug into his shoulder as her back arched, her wet hair sliding against his chin. He looked down at her chest. Her nipples were tiny buds. He longed for them to be in his mouth. Firm peaks as he flicked his tongue back and forth over her sweet, hot flesh.

Fantasies he could never make reality.

His chest rose in gasps against her trembling frame. Air wasn't enough. He wanted to breathe *her* in.

Miranda's weight pushed into the center of his chest, right where he was trying to catch his breath, and he lost it a moment. The distraction allowed her to dig her fingers into the back of the hand between her legs and force them down.

To her entrance.

The tips of his fingers dipped into her hot channel.

His eyes flashed wide, and pleasure exploded in his cock as it pulsed against her ass.

The entry of his fingers was so fucking *easy*.

"Please," she said, panting. Breasts rising and falling. Nipples taut and beckoning. "*Govek.*"

He shuddered, pleasure blooming in his gut, spiraling up his spine. Even through the gloves, he could feel how slick she was. How hard she was pulsing.

She was ready to go off.

And this would be over.

And she would realize *what* she'd given her body to.

Fuck, it was too soon. *He wanted more.*

He slipped his fingers out of her, relishing the sensation of her tightness easing away. Wondering if he could slow this down. He slid his thumb and index finger against each other, slick despite the water.

For him.

Fuck.

He wasn't ready. But she was. And he couldn't pretend he didn't know that anymore.

"Govek." His name on her lips blazed through his mind. His cock jerked against her ass. Her hand moved down past his. He craned his neck to watch, his throat tight. She dipped her finger into her channel, thrusting all the way to her knuckle. Groaning. He quivered at the sinful sight.

"I want to. . ." His fingers trembled with the need to spear her, thrust deep into her. Bring her off against him.

And then this would be over, and he would have to face her and she would look at him with utter *revulsion*, and . . . fuck. *Fuck.*

"I'll do it if you don't." She reached up to grip his hand, clasping his two fingers and pulling them down.

That threat was enough for him.

Fades be fucked if he'd let her take this from him.

"Fine," he managed through clenched teeth and gave into her completely.

CHAPTER

ELEVEN

"That's it, tough guy," Miranda whispered under her breath, bringing her hand up to brush her fingers along Govek's jaw as he finally relaxed behind her. She was so worked up she could hardly stand it. Her whole body was in agony from being on the cusp for so long. Her clit was pounding so hard she felt it all the way up in her stomach.

She was too sensitive, overstimulated. She hadn't ever dreamed that being with another person could be so much better than touching herself.

But it was. And Govek was too sexy and raw and *good* at what he was doing and not going fast enough for her.

Moving both hands down to clasp his fingers, she forced his hand into the position she wanted. Two fingers up, the rest curled under. He obeyed, allowing himself to be pliable.

"Miranda," Govek warned, and goddamn him, his voice was like a caress all on its own. Like a vibrator for her whole body. She was convinced she wouldn't be so strung up if he couldn't tremble need into her with nothing but a broken word.

"Oh, Govek," she said, forcing him to hiss into her ear. She wished she could turn to look at him, but the delicious grip he had on her cheek, her chin, was too tight. Soaking his heat deep into her brain. Muddling up her senses.

She wanted more.

He huffed loudly, the exhale warming her damp scalp.

"Like this, I just need . . ." When he didn't move fast enough, she worked his hand lower. His two fingers grazed through her slick pussy.

Her squirming body was aching for the sting of his massive fingers stretching her tight. It would drown out the overwhelming ache in her clit. Tamp out the oversensitivity.

Miranda's insistence was finally enough and Govek rubbed over her sensitive flesh, pressing into her entrance. Slick digits speared inside with little resistance. She lost her breath. One second, she was empty and the next she was pulsing tight around him.

Govek's breath hitched, trembled.

The stretch was incredible, and he worked deeper, spearing into her. The rough texture of the glove and the heat of his massive palm covering her clit made her back arch and her body quiver.

Miranda thrust her hips up, trying to get him into the right position so she could take more. It had been an easier task with her toys, but his subtle twitching was so much better. It was all him. His passion, his lust, his want to please her. Each little involuntary jerk and pulse had her babbling.

"Oh, Govek, yes. That's good." She stroked his palm. "Curl your fingers a little and press up."

He made a strangled noise, and she wished he would just give in and *moan* already. Growl at her. Make demands. *Something*. Why was he so quiet?

Then his strong fingers skewered right into her G-spot.

"Oh *fuck*," she wailed, grinding on him. Her pussy gushed around his hand. "Th-that's it. Keep doing *that*."

Govek's stuttered out a wheezy, disbelieving laugh. As if he couldn't believe she could take so much of him. That she was growing wetter from what he was doing.

She might have been the virgin here, but he was clearly far less experienced.

What if he was a virgin, too?

Miranda twisted, shivered, and rolled her hips. She imagined all the things she would introduce to him. Fuck, if he was a virgin, he'd probably never gotten a blowjob, and she'd never given one, but that didn't stop her from ringing out her pleasure, envisioning his bliss-wrecked face as she rocked his world.

He'd look so fucking good while she sucked his massive cock. Flicked her tongue from base to tip. Played out all her own fantasies on him while he writhed and growled.

She wanted to see him so badly right now.

As if he could read her mind, Govek leaned in close and buried his nose in her hair. Dragging her scent into his lungs so hard, she felt like he was breathing in her soul.

"Do I smell good, tough guy?" She begged him to speak as she pushed his hand to keep thrusting. Her question ended in a deep moan that bloomed from the bottom of her quivering stomach.

"*Yes*." His voice was rough in her ear. Heat raged through her veins and pulsed in her pussy. "So, fucking good, Miranda."

"Oh god." She picked up speed and fucked his fingers harder, and they slipped deeper into her core.

His long, thick digit pressed into her G-spot. The ecstasy seared through her veins, up and down her spine. Unrelenting, maddening. She twisted, and bucked, and he flicked hard and fast into that sensitive spot. Bliss roared behind her eyes, skittering up her spine. She yanked her knees from his hold, brought them up, and clenched her thighs around his hand, forcing him even deeper.

Right where she needed him.

He stretched her taut and her breath seized, her nerves danced. Bliss licked down her limbs. Her muscles flexed as the pleasure mounted, tingling in her gut. She needed more, more, *more*.

Her pussy tightened. She was on the precipice. Her lungs constricted and light burst behind her eyes.

His palm swirled against her clit. His fingers pushed deep, stroked hard.

She shattered, orgasm exploding against his fingers. Pussy dripping and pulsing, like a vice. Trapping him as she clenched her thighs around his hand.

"Govek, *ooh*!" Torturous waves of rapture coursed through her, strung her out, and twisted her raw emotions.

"Fuck, woman," Govek's voice grated into her hair, ringing her out even more. Pushing her past the limit. Drawing the orgasm out so long and harsh, she was almost convulsing.

She clung to his hand, bunching the glove in her fist as the bliss faded and euphoria took its place. She went limp against his chest, dragging hard won air into her lungs, and feeling drowsy. The sound of Govek's harsh breathing, the feel of his chest rising and falling under her, added a contentment she'd never felt when she'd done this alone.

Govek rumbled a pleased sound, pulling her up, bathing her in his warmth.

By god, did she ever want to see him! She wanted to strip him bare and touch him. Turn around and give him as much pleasure as he'd just given her.

But she needed a little more time to recover. Her muscles felt numb and floppy, and she wanted to rest in his arms for a couple more minutes.

She was so fricking selfish.

Govek nuzzled her again, purred into her ear. "Good, woman. Relax for me."

Apparently, he didn't seem to care that she wasn't reciprocating. He loosened his grip on her face slightly so she could lean toward him and press her scalp into his cheek.

It was just her and him, surrounded by the pool. Lazy and warm. Content.

A low wail sounded from the forest beyond.

Miranda froze, gripping Govek and straining to hear. That sound couldn't be back again . . . it wasn't—

"Miranda?" Govek brought her about by her shoulders, still not quite letting her turn.

He really didn't want her to see him. The confusion of that had her fidgeting with the edge of his glove. His hot hand was still between her legs, cupping her pulsing pussy. Distracting her from the unsettling forest sounds that were absolutely her imagination. They couldn't be real. It was just her overtaxed brain trying to ruin this.

"I'm fine," she assured him, and Govek slowly relaxed in response.

It was in her head. She *was* fine. Everything was okay.

Govek let out a little huff and Miranda, desperate for more distraction, continued her praise. "I'm amazing. Perfect. That was incredible. It's so much better with you than by myself."

He rumbled contentedly, and her stomach pooled with heat all over again. Lacing a tingling bliss through her limbs. She wished she could see his face, but made do with trailing her fingers down his bulging arms. One hand still possessively cupping her sex. The other tight on her hip, holding her captive.

She could feel his cock still rock solid against her back, and she squirmed her hips against it.

"Miranda." His voice rumbled low and sweet, shuddering bliss up her spine.

The siren wailed again.

Miranda froze. The deep drone was closer now. Just beyond the trees.

It couldn't be denied.

Her heart began a frantic rhythm. Her muscles bunched, readying to bolt.

"Thank you for this boon, Miranda."

The wail continued, sucking her under. She tried to fight. It wasn't real. It wasn't there.

"There is . . . another position you could take for me . . . since conquest does not suit you."

What was he saying? She wanted to ask him to repeat, but her mind was split, straining to hear the siren.

And it came again. Spiking through her. Shivering up her spine. Govek released her slightly in response. Letting his limbs drop to her sides in the water.

"If . . ." Govek continued speaking, though his words

seemed far away. As if he were calling her from the other end of a dark tunnel. "If you want . . ."

Her ears vibrated. It was so close now, wailing and bubbling up. It ripped through the trees and screamed its warning. It could not be denied.

Miranda knew it better than any other.

An air raid was coming.

"You might take me as your ma—"

Govek's voice was drowned out by the growing scream of a siren as it exploded right next to her head. Terror forced her to quiver. The desperation to find a hiding place slammed her in the gut. It was an instinctual drive. Born from a lifetime of practice drills.

"You need not decide now . . ." Govek spoke again, and his voice was even further away. Distorted through a long tunnel.

No. Not a tunnel. A metal tube.

The air vent.

Darkness closed around her, screaming its threat. Bringing death. Heat. Crunching metal.

Miranda bolted.

She sprang from the water, leaping toward the bank. Out of the spring. Onto the sand.

She needed to find shelter. Now.

The bombs were coming again.

The siren's scream was so *loud*.

She couldn't get away.

She was being dragged. Yanked back by the arm.

By Mr. Barker.

He was shoving her down the bank steps. Into the vault.

She had to get away, she had to hide. She had to escape him.

He was going to lock her up alone again.

Underground.

She would suffocate this time. She would scream and bash herself bloody.

She was drowning. The torturous dark flooding down her throat.

There were horrors in that dark.

Horrors she couldn't remember.

She didn't want to remember.

But she had to.

She ran blindly. Her panic was relentless. Her lungs were heaving.

But she could not escape.

CHAPTER

TWELVE

Miranda bolted.

She slapped his hands away and dragged herself through the water.

Govek slashed to catch her, but froze when his claws came too close to her perfect skin.

He dragged air into his nose and unhinged his jaw to scent for threats.

There was nothing.

Nothing to trigger her terror.

Except for him.

He'd told her he would hunt her if she ran from him. She was a fool. A wretched beautiful fool.

Yerina had never been so stupid to run like this. She'd known what would happen if she did.

Miranda didn't.

And after the raging fire Miranda had built in his bones, he had no control.

Govek bounded into action, leaping to the bank to chase his woman down. His muscles blazed and his blood boiled and his instincts drove him mad.

Miranda's steps were skittering and strange, as if she were running blindly. She tripped on a rock and went down hard enough to make him flinch. Then she got back up and continued as if she hadn't even noticed.

She did not look back as he pounded up behind her. He cut her off before she made it out of the sand, leaping into her path. She did not recoil as he raged for her to halt.

Still she ran.

Straight into him.

She stumbled, and he caught her before she could plummet to the ground. She barely fought him as he lowered her to the sandy beach and caged her beneath him. His legs pinned her hips, his hands gripped her shoulders, so she couldn't even squirm.

He knew she would reject him. This was the way it always was. It was the natural course of things. And then he would win her back in a few days' time with boons and patience and a careful concealing of everything that made him vile.

His father's voice blazed in his mind, *"You must control yourself, Govek. The mates of our clan fear you too much. You will chase them away."*

Miranda wouldn't even *look* at him.

And he had no fucking boons.

Miranda hadn't even told him what she wanted. At least Yerina always *told* him what would quell her disgust and gave him hope that he could win her back.

Until he couldn't anymore. Until he had nothing left to give.

He had nothing *now*.

Why had he ever believed Miranda could be different?

"Let me out. Oh god. Don't leave me here!"

Govek stilled. *Don't leave her?*

"Oh god, oh god. I can't get out. I'm trapped." She was panting the words, whispering them on the wind, and she wouldn't meet his eyes.

"Miranda," he said in a demanding tone. She didn't flinch.

She was not *here*. She was inside her mind, caught in a horror.

He'd seen this with Karthoc's orcs when they'd traveled to Clairton. The terrors of their past had gripped them so tightly they relived it. The others had bellowed in their faces, forced them out of it by way of rage and harshness.

He raised his voice. "Miranda!"

She cowered, and he gritted his teeth. He could not bellow at her that way.

"Let me out! Let me out, *please*—"

"You are out, Miranda." He moved back slightly so he wasn't crowding her. "You are out."

"Don't leave me." Her hands clawed at his bare chest, and he relished the sensation. She was trying to cling *to* him, not get away.

Blast, he was sick. She was lying naked and vulnerable, caught in her past agonies, and he was relieved she wasn't rejecting him.

"I'm not leaving. You belong with me, Miranda. You are my . . ." Fuck, what should he even call her?

"G-Govek?"

"Yes." He was lost to the haunted flickering in her gaze.

Her fingers clung to him, and he moved closer until he could feel her breath fanning his flesh.

She touched his forehead, trailed her fingertips down his cheeks over and over until he was panting. Her eyes darted from his to the forest. "The siren."

"What?" he rasped, dizzy from her touch. She was still stroking him.

"To . . . to warn of the attack. So, we can get to safety."

Attacks? Hiding? "Speak more, Miranda. I don't understand."

Her lips trembled. Tears streaked across her cheeks. "I . . . I heard a warning siren."

Had she imagined it? "There was no warning, Miranda."

She gulped. "But I heard . . . I heard . . ."

She'd heard something or imagined it. Tension ebbed out of him. "I thought you were rejecting me."

Her eyes widened as she snapped to attention. "What?"

"I thought . . . I thought you were running away from me."

Gentle fingers played in his hair, smoothing it. She trailed down to his nape. "I wouldn't. I'm not. You don't scare me."

His breath huffed in a disbelieving snort.

Her eyes misted over again, and he went cold. "But I am scared."

He froze, heaved air. She curled into his chest, her bare body pressing into him and whispered, "I'm so scared, Govek."

The words broke him, left him crumbling under the storm of his own terrors.

Tavggol was gone. His father had ordered him to his death. His clan had abandoned him.

His world was blighted and dying.

Miranda's warmth pressed into his chest, his cheek, and squeezed around his neck.

He moved down into her willing, eager embrace. She wrapped both arms and legs around him and nestled closer.

She clung to him like he was her Fades-given miracle and not the other way around.

"I'm scared." Her voice broke, and he felt it to the pit of his soul.

Me too, Govek thought as he crushed her to him. He was so fucking scared. They were in this dread together, sinking side by side.

He held Miranda for so long he forgot where they were and the dangers that lurked.

Slowly, he sat up, though only far enough to see her face. Fades help him. She was a vision. Her eyes were clear, and her breathing was back to a steady rhythm. He wanted to bury himself in her neck and drink up the scent of her.

She smelled so fucking good.

"Can I pick you up?" he asked, voice thick.

She nodded, and he lifted her effortlessly, trying to keep the motion smooth. It was a difficult task with her clinging to him so tightly, but he managed to get her to the boulder she'd left her cloak and shorts on.

"I'm sorry," she whispered as she tucked her face into his shoulder. The sincerity in her tone made him ache. "I kinda lost it there, huh? I don't . . . know what happened." Her smile faltered, as if she were about to weep again.

He gripped her soft calf in his hand and drew her leg out, brushed the sand from it. She squirmed as he gave the other the same attention, and then he moved up to her torso and her back. He kept his gaze averted from her as best he could, but his eyes were drawn to every curve and her still bare breasts. His hands twitched at the memory of how soft and full they were in his hands.

Fuck, he was a beast.

"I'm so sorry." Her voice cracked, and he flinched, jerking his eyes back to her face. "I really don't know why I ran like that."

Her breathing was deep and slow as he tucked her cloak around her bare shoulders, protecting her from the forest chill. "It is fine, Miranda. You were just lost in a horror."

She went lax, and her expression of utter gratitude overwhelmed him. "That simple, huh?"

"Yes."

Her lips trembled. "I don't know what happened to me. On Earth. I can't remember some of it . . . a lot of it. I should be dead. I shouldn't have survived it."

Govek gulped, the mention of her death making the imprint rage in his veins. He tried to hide it, swallow it down. She needed his aid now but he was uncertain of what he could do to quell her fear.

But at least he could help her get warm. "You should get dressed." He crossed the beach to get the underwear and breast covering she'd thrown at him. The sun had done little to dry them, and they were basically tatters, but he brought them back to her nonetheless.

She took them and he started back toward his pack, determined to find her something more to wear. He glanced toward the still steaming pool where he had just wrung out her pleasure and gulped.

Miranda let out a little whimper, and he whipped his head back to her. She'd put on her underwear and was fidgeting with the strap of her tight-fitting top. It clung to her breasts even more now that it was wet. She grimaced, forcing him to ask, "What is wrong?"

"Just . . . cold," she said, touching the wet breast covering right over her nipples.

Full, rosy-tipped breasts, plump in his hands.

Fuck, he was vile for thinking about this while she was still recovering.

She shivered again and her discomfort flooded dismay into his marrow, making the imprint roar to life.

Her face suddenly paled, and he feared she may lose consciousness. He rushed back to her side.

"Oh god! There it is again!" Miranda was trembling, terrified.

Reaching for him, she brought her hands to his chest as he instinctively curled around her, caging her in.

Fades, she clung to him in her fear. She was not running away, and she was looking to him for comfort. The imprint *roared*.

She stared off into the forest, searching.

"What, Miranda?"

"That! That siren. The air raid—I . . . I mean the warning sound. That! You know, *that*." She somehow managed to squiggle closer, pressing her whole torso into his. "That sound. That sound right there. What the fuck is that? It's not—"

"That's a riabell." There were no other sounds except the rustling of wind in the leaves, so she must have been referring to the riabell's low call.

"A-a what? What is it?"

"A bird."

She went still, eyes huge but focused. She was not lost to him this time.

He squeezed her. "It's a bird call. Can I lift you again?" She was already wrapping her arms around his neck before he finished the question. His flesh tingled with the contact.

He carried her part way into the woods, careful with each step and noise, scanning the tree canopy until he finally found his target. "There," he pointed to the white bird nestled in the branches above. "That is a riabell. They enjoy hunting for fish in the springs."

Miranda stared at the large creature. It was half as tall as her, with a long beak and longer legs.

"It looks like a heron," she said softly. "But they're extinct. Not enough clean water and food and—"

She broke off, flinching as it gave a low cry. The sound started deep and built higher before trailing off.

"Dang." She raked a hand over her face. "That's horrible."

"Riabell's are considered a good omen," Govek said carefully. "Stories say that they lead lost travelers out of the forests or guide hunters to elk herds."

"You get lost in the woods?" she asked skeptically.

He huffed in amusement, "No."

Miranda curled around his neck and he closed his eyes, relishing the sensation of her warmth as she willingly cleaved to him. He was certain he would never grow accustomed to it.

"Then I guess you don't need guidance."

"Riabell's guide humans, not orcs."

"Fine, *I* don't need guidance then. I've got you for that, right?"

"Yes," he soothed, taking her hint. He jerked his arm

toward the creature, startling it into flight. It rose above the canopy with brilliant bursts of its wings and disappeared.

His woman relaxed slowly, rewarding him with a deep sigh and a caress to the back of his neck. "Th-thank you."

He nodded, returning her to the spring, pondering on her description of the bird's call. A warning siren. What in her world needed such warnings? And why was it so terrible that it caused her mind to fracture?

Her world exploded. What could cause such devastation?

His throat tightened, but he would not prod. It would do no good and he did not want to dim his relief.

She had not fled because he'd scared her or disgusted her. Or even because he'd admitted his longing to take her as a mate.

Which meant . . . would she consider it?

He set her down on the same stone and gave her a good once over. She was no worse for wear. A little sandy still. He brushed the rest of it off her arms and sides and out of her wet hair.

He tried to keep to the task of checking her over, searching for any cuts or bruises on her tender flesh. But his mind kept returning to those precious, incredible moments they'd had in the spring.

To think, a few days prior he'd been certain of his swift death at the hands of the Waking Order.

"Govek?"

Miranda's sweet voice drew him from his thoughts. She wrapped her bare feet around his legs and stroked her toes up the back of his thighs. "You okay?"

Fuck! That should not feel so good. And she should not smell so fucking sweet so soon after she'd had a release. It should have taken half a moon, at least before she was willing to receive him again. Half a moon and a mountain of fox furs and berries and even a few tinctures for good measure.

But it hadn't. The honeyed scent of her could not be denied.

He did not deserve such bliss. "Where are your shoes, woman?"

She gestured to the ground, and he huffed with embarrassment that he hadn't noticed her shoes right at his feet. Other than the shoes, which were strangely intricate, she also had a pair of tiny trousers that may as well have been a blasted handkerchief. The useless scrap of filthy fabric was better left abandoned on the rock.

Govek went to retrieve his own abandoned slacks, cloak, and pack, and returned to her. "Are you hungry?"

"Always." Her voice was husky from screaming, but the tone was lighter. She was overcoming the darkness more swiftly than he expected.

She was strong. His chest swelled with pride.

He handed her some dried elk meat and more hard bread. He would need to hunt for her soon.

"I have your bag here. Do you want anything from it?" he asked, after searching through his things and finding her blue pack tucked near the bottom. Did she have any extra clothes within it?

Her brow pinched. "No. I don't want it. God, to think I'm polluting your world with plastic. That stuff should have stayed on Earth."

Govek didn't know what plastic was, but it didn't matter. She clearly missed some aspects of her fallen world, and one day, she may want these few remnants. He would keep them until she did. He shoved the blue bag back to the bottom of his pack, out of the way.

He'd found his extra shirt when her voice broke. "Was this . . . meant for someone else?"

Glancing up, he found her fumbling with the edge of the cloak, eyes wary, as if worried what his response might be. "What?"

"It isn't big enough for you. Did you bring it for someone in particular?"

Catching her discomfort, he said, "I made it for you."

She blinked, eyes huge. "What?"

Govek considered taking back his words, but he examined the fit of the cloak, the smooth set of the shoulders, the length that covered down to her ankle without dragging on the ground, the width that would allow for her slight frame to fill out some.

The blasted thing fit her fucking *perfect.* Like the Fades had guided his hand with her in mind while he cut and stitched it.

"I made it for you, Miranda." He gripped the hood, hands moving to the sides of her face. Her cheeks were pink as he pulled it up. Her skull filled it out so it couldn't fall in front of her eyes.

He lost his reservations for the briefest moment and trailed his still gloved hands along the rim of her ears. She shivered and leaned into the touch. Warmth bloomed in him.

"For you." His voice was barely a whisper. "My . . ." mate. He wanted to say it so badly, but the image of her bolting from him was too sharp. Even if he now knew that wasn't why she'd fled.

Her breath fanned his face.

Her soft lips brushed his cheek.

She kissed him. She willingly kissed him without the barest hint of prompting. Heat spiked from the lingering touch and radiated throughout his chest.

"Thank you, Govek," she said, and he felt as if he would burst apart. "I don't know where I would be without . . . well, I guess I do know. It wouldn't be good." She leaned in and kissed his cheek *again* and tightly clung to his neck. "I have no idea how I'm going to pay you back, but I swear I will. If you ever think of something I could do . . ."

Fuck! He was a greedy wretch, but he would not pass up this offer. "You must stay with me then."

She leaned back to meet his gaze.

He swallowed hard. "Stay with me until . . . until I can think of a way for you to repay me."

Her lips quirked and the barest hint of a chuckle left them. It skewered him, drawing him back into those moments she'd rolled with laughter while bathing. The incredible sound was more gorgeous than anything he could have possibly imagined.

"All right," she agreed. "I'll do that."

She'd finished the food, so he offered the water pouch. She took slow sips before continuing. "Thanks for coming after me, too. I probably would be in Timbuktu by now if you hadn't snapped me out of it. Or whatever place is super far from here. I'm not usually like that . . . I've never . . ." She took a deep breath, gulping hard.

"I told you I would chase you, and I will do it again if you try to flee." He pulled the extra shirt he had out of his pack and shook it out.

Her smile returned. "I know you mean that like a threat, but it doesn't feel like one." He stilled. "Maybe we should try it out sometime."

His blood heated as pleasure danced in his veins. The image of her darting away from him, laughing as he raced after her, hair billowing behind her, with cheeks and lips red, chest heaving.

While he fucking *chased* her? Hunted her down?

Fuck.

He shook for control. "For Fades' sake, put on the fucking shirt so we can get moving."

"Yes, sir," she conceded, handing him back the pouch. "Should we fill that with more spring water? What if you get hurt again?"

He would fill it here, but . . . "The healing effect diminishes with distance and time. By the morn, it will have no magic left."

"Oh," she said, seeming a bit disappointed. His heart twinged. Was she worried about him?

She tucked the shirt he'd given her beneath her cloak so she could put it on. It drowned her, the arms baggy and rolled to fit the length of hers. The neckline dipped so low he could see the top of her breast covering. It bunched at her hips, far too long to suit her torso. She gently stroked the buttons he'd made himself. "I think I'll just use the extra fabric to tie it up."

He turned his attention to digging through his pack for more clothing, even though he knew he had nothing. She needed something to cover her legs.

"Man, I'm going to look like something else when we finally get to where we're going. Not that I'm complaining." She rushed on. "I'm super grateful. I just . . ." she plucked at the oversized shirt, smirking down at how baggy it was.

Govek huffed, thinking it looked good on her, regardless.

"Where *are* we going, by the way?"

He paused his search.

"I mean, I don't know anything about your world. Is it all forests like this? Are there towns too? Civilization and . . ."

"There are villages of humans and clans of orcs. Goblins have retreated deep into their mines and sylphs live high in the mountains and have not been seen for decades," he said, half distracted. He'd just gone over every possession he owned. There were nowhere near enough medical tinctures. No blankets or furs to keep the cold away. No extra food to keep her hale.

Fuck! What was he going to do? Where *would* they go? Karthoc's forge was much too far, and the nearer orc clans were at war. They could run right into *battle* if he wasn't careful.

But he would not, he *could* not, return to Rove Wood Clan. It was not an option. He would *have* to think of something else. *Anything* else.

His claws extended in the gloves and he feared he might shred them, but he couldn't control himself. A deep simmer of rage bubbled in his gut.

"Govek? I'll follow you anywhere. And I can help you too. Kinda. If you show me herbs to hunt down, I could try to find them. I could learn to start fires and gut fish."

He wasn't going to be able to provide for her. Not like this.

"Not sure I'll ever be as good at *catching* fish as you, but I can try. And you really don't have to hunt for me. I'm more than happy to live off fish and plants. Though . . . I guess there aren't very many foraging options right now. Your planet is going into winter, right?"

Govek breathed deep, worked for calm and logic. There was a cave near here. An old entry to the goblin mines, long abandoned, but that was only a temporary option. It would not serve them through the harsh winter.

"Sorry, I'll try to shut up now," she murmured, jarring him out of his thoughts.

"You may speak as much as you like, Miranda," he assured her, though it came out too harsh.

She fidgeted on the rock. "I know it's too much. Sometimes it just . . . stops my brain, you know?"

"If I wanted to stop my brain, sleep would be my preferred method," he stated, earning a chuckle from her.

"Sleep, huh?" She narrowed her eyes at him, a sly smile striking up his longing. "I can think of something else that could keep us both nice and distracted."

Fuck. He gulped hard, moving closer to her. Desperate for whatever pleasure she was willing to gift him. His mind grappled with what boons he had on hand to give her to keep her lust high.

He picked up his damp slacks. "I'm going to give you these."

"I was joking earlier about stealing your clothes," she said. "I mean, not that I don't want you to strut around naked."

"I will give you my underwear too if you want them, Miranda." He grumbled low, causing her to blush. It was too easy.

Then her gaze raked down his body, and he gulped.

"Oh, wow," she whispered in a reverent tone.

Miranda's jaw was slack, and her gaze lingered on his

groin, at the outline where his cock lay tucked beneath his undergarments, semi-hard and aching. She bit her lower lip and his blood simmered.

"Fuck me . . ." She breathed under her breath.

Heat speared him. Was that a request?

She lustfully moved her gaze from his groin to his chest, then his face. "Are you sure you're real?"

He was afraid to move less he startle her and ruin this. He'd never felt such hungry eyes upon him before.

"Come over here," she said and jerked him forward until she could rest her hands against his sides. She guided him to stand between her legs.

He lost his breath.

She gifted him with a hint of a smile before reaching up to tug his head down to her level. She lingered her lips on his cheek, just as sweet and potent as her first kiss had been. He held still, willing her to remain for a few moments longer.

Miranda moved off, and it felt like the sun had set on him.

Then her lips found his mouth.

Electric pleasure danced down his spine. Her incredible honey scent burst and muddled his thoughts. Her mouth fit perfectly between his fangs. Plump soft lips teasing his own. His heart was skittering at such a rapid pace he thought it might spark.

She drifted away far too soon and searched his face. Then she quirked a fucking adorable smile.

"Okay?"

"Fuck yes," he growled. The rumble came straight from his chest and reverberated with the same tempo as his frantic heartbeat.

She'd *kissed* him. On the mouth. Between his fangs and tusks. She had to have felt them on her cheeks and still she'd done it. He couldn't fucking believe it.

His breath left in a rush before she bridged the gap and claimed his lips again. Barely brushing. She was so fucking gentle, and he wanted her to scorch him with her mouth. Brand him as her own.

He dragged her essence into his lungs and almost collapsed. He couldn't believe his own senses, but her scent was unmistakable. Raw and rich and wanting him all over again.

She truly was attracted to him. *Him.* A hulking, unsightly orc who was despised by his own kin. Confusion made him growl into her mouth.

And her desire intensified. Tension shot up his back as she squirmed and pressed closer.

His growling had heightened her arousal, and he was *fucking losing his mind.*

He broke away this time. "You want me again."

Her eyes were huge, and her breath caught.

Uncertainty drove him to snarl. "You want me?"

She gulped, licking her sweet lips with her tongue, and she nodded.

"Fuck." He clumsily forced his pants off and shoved her feet into the legs. They drowned her but he managed to pull them up around her waist and tie the drawstring with shaking fingers.

He would take her to the goblin caves. They weren't far. After—once he had his blasted senses back—he would be able to logic through where they would go next. He threw his pack onto his shoulder.

"Govek?" Miranda was breathless as she allowed him to

scoop her up into his arms. "Where . . . where are we going now?"

"To privacy," he said, earning a blush from her before she hid herself in his neck. Her embarrassment spiked deep yearning in him.

He would enjoy ridding her of it.

THIRTEEN

MIRANDA

"Woman, you must tell me why you refuse to enter." Miranda shivered at the mouth of the cavern Govek had revealed behind a curtain of vines. The sun was slowly setting, casting this world into an eerie twilight. Deep shadows pitched the cave into darkness and concealed the opposite end.

The entry was a sliver. Barely big enough for Govek to squeeze through sideways.

Miranda's heels dug into the dirt, refusing to move.

It was not a bank vault. She was in a forest. It was okay. She could get past this. Overcome it. Push it to the back of her mind where the suffocating squeeze of metal couldn't—

Govek's warm hand gripped her shoulder. His opposite hand balanced a spear-like branch with five fish.

He'd caught them on the way, just a few hours ago. His muscles had been outlined in the sunlight, his green skin had been glistening and damp.

Miranda fought for reason, to focus on Govek. He was a brilliant distraction. The best. And they would need to cook those fish soon or they might go bad. But her mind lurched its way back to the cave. No matter of logic could convince her to enter.

He leaned in to meet her eyes. "Miranda, speak or I cannot provide a remedy."

She licked her lips. Govek's hot flesh on her chilly nape anchored her to the forest. Miranda sidled a little closer to him, soaking up every drop of comfort he offered and locked all her trauma behind a crumbling wall in her mind.

"Miranda," Govek demanded again. "Speak, woman."

"It's too small," she managed. The skepticism on his face would have made her laugh under any other circumstances. "The door. I mean, the opening."

This time, his bafflement made her chuckle. She was being stupid, but the idea of going inside this cave with only a tiny crack to escape made her skin prickle and her legs itched to bolt, no matter what pleasures this orc promised her within.

He propped the spear of fish against a nearby rock and turned to examine the rock wall for a moment, brow furrowed. Then went back to her.

"Can I pick you up, Miranda?"

"Oh, uh. Yeah. Okay." He swooped her off her feet almost before she finished speaking. He carried her to a rock ten or more feet away, plunked her down on top, and tucked her cloak around her. His fingers briefly grazed her scalp before darting away.

He was so careful when he touched her. It made her chest ache.

"Stay here," he demanded, before stalking back over to

the cave. He placed a hand on the massive, moss-covered boulder to the left of the opening. It was fatter than he was tall, and partially buried in the soft, leaf covered ground.

"What are you doing?" She sounded a bit alarmed as he reached up to throw a few of the smaller rocks on top of the boulder off to the side. It caused a cascade of dust and rubble to fall onto his shoulders. "Be careful!"

All he did was shoot her an amused look and cover his head with the hood of his cloak. Then he leveraged his weight against the boulder and heaved.

The dang thing moved. Actually *rolled*.

Miranda squirmed as Govek's muscles bulged in his arms. His expression was tight and focused. He growled—the sound spiked heat right through her bones—and gave a tremendous shove before bolting out of the way. Rocks rained down where he'd been, and Miranda yelped with surprise.

Govek gave an appraising look at his work and brushed off his hands as if he'd just casually bucked a bale of hay. "There. Will that do?"

She'd been so concerned about his safety, she hadn't noticed what he'd done. Which was substantially open up the mouth of the cave. Five feet of space now spanned the passageway.

"My god, Govek," she breathed, waving him over to her while she examined the boulder he'd moved. It had left a hole in the ground the size of a bathtub. "Just how much weight *can* you lift?"

He snorted, stopping in front of her. "I could not lift that boulder, Miranda. I only pushed it."

"Semantics," she muttered, reaching to brush the rubble from his cloak and take off his hood. "Are you okay?"

He quirked a brow. "Yes. Will you enter now?"

She took a deep breath and nodded, but even as he helped her down and walked her over, she found herself asking, "We won't get trapped in there, will we?"

"No, Miranda," Govek assured her without hesitation, as he placed his massive hand on her lower back and pressed her into the cave. "I will not allow us to become trapped," he arranged the vines so they covered the larger entryway.

"I guess you could just push down that whole side and get us free," Miranda said, gesturing to the front wall, only half joking.

Govek turned and flashed her a smile. An actual *smile*. Miranda's heart thundered right off the rock face and smacked the ground as hard as the boulder had. Dang! He looked flipping *fine* when he was smiling.

He stepped further in and lowered his pack to the ground, murmuring, "I would turn this whole hillside to rubble if you willed it, Miranda. Though that would defeat the purpose of having a safe place to be alone."

She approached him, and his smile faded into blinking shock. She pulled him down so she could kiss his cheek, his warm skin soft under her lips, the husky scent of him deeply comforting. "My hero."

Her tone was a little more reverent than she intended, and Govek's jaw dropped, revealing many sharp teeth. Teeth she craved to trace with her tongue.

Oh, frick, she was a goner. If Govek knew, he'd probably already have her bent over that boulder he'd pushed aside. Or at least she hoped he would.

He sucked in a breath and offered her the water before going about the task of building a fire in one of the stone circles.

The space was quite roomy, actually. At least thirty feet in diameter with rough stone walls and a semi-smooth floor. It wasn't a natural cave, rather it had been carved out of the hillside by hand to create an ovular structure. The entry had been built with stones and boulders stacked to look natural, but upon closer inspection, Miranda saw they couldn't have been. It was too perfect to be done by nature alone.

There were a few circular fire pits made from old rocks, which were the only indication that anyone had ever spent time here before.

"Whose cave is this?" she asked.

"Goblins."

Her spine straightened. "Aren't they the guys who poisoned you?"

"Yes, but *they* did not poison me. Humans did. Using goblin poison." He continued gathering debris to use as firewood. "Goblins abandoned this cave long ago. They no longer come to the surface."

"Are . . . they friendly?" She wrung her hands, still wrapping her brain around orcs.

He shrugged. "The three sentinel races are at peace with one another. We cannot afford war among each other as well as the Waking Order."

She nodded as he struck up the fire with wet twigs. "How did you know this place was here?"

"I stayed here once, with a party of other orcs." He said this so casually, but it had Miranda reeling.

What did he mean by a party of other orcs? Who were his family? Where was his clan? What was his upbringing like?

"Miranda."

She looked up to find Govek had finished arranging the

fish to roast and was now staring at her. His eyes reflected the firelight. She lost every question she'd planned to ask as her gut heated deliciously.

Miranda pulled her cloak off and laid it out by the fire before sitting down on top of it.

"Wanna sit by me?" she offered, scooching over to make room for him on the cloak. Though it wasn't much room.

He turned around, still watching her, looking like he might pounce. Her stomach flipped and fluttered, and she chewed her lips.

He kneeled near her, though not on the cloak, his gaze on her hair. He reached out but stopped short of touching her.

"It's kinda wavy, huh?" she said breathlessly. "It's nice, actually. I can usually just brush it and let it do what it wants, and it looks good." She'd taken advantage of that many, *many* times when she pulled a daycare shift before work started at the bank.

"You are the loveliest thing I have ever seen, Miranda."

All traces of humor died out in her chest at the husky way his voice rumbled over her. She broke the eye contact, feeling overwhelmed. "That's a really sweet thing to say to someone who just survived the apocalypse."

Govek's brows rose, and for one staggering moment, Miranda thought he might ask. That she might finally get into this.

She wasn't ready, though. She wasn't sure she would *ever* be ready to relive what had happened to her on Earth. The emotional tide rose in the back of her throat and it was all she could do to keep it locked away. Out of sight.

"Miranda."

Govek's voice brought her back, and she blinked rapidly

at him. "S-sorry, were you saying something? I swear I'm not so spacey on a normal day. I can multitask like none other. You have to, to take care of a group of toddlers all by yourself." Her throat closed, and she choked on the words. Frick! She was trying *not* to think about this, and now it was all she could do.

Her babies were all she could see.

"Hmm." A gentle brush through her hair brought her back to the present. Govek ran his gloved fingers slowly across her temple and back behind her ear. The leather pushed through the strands and felt cool on her cheek.

He wrapped a hand around the base of her skull and pulled her forward into his chest. The swift scent of pine and the heat of his skin soothed her like something out of her best daydreams. The lull of his heart thrummed a quiet rhythm into her muscles. His breath, against the top of her head, tickled her hair and forced her eyes to flutter.

She took a deep breath, soaking up the sensation of being surrounded by him. Just like when he'd caught her in the sand.

It was so easy to forget everything when Govek wrapped her up like this. And she *wanted* to forget. It hurt too much.

Why had she survived when everyone else was gone?

Why couldn't she save them?

"Hush," Govek whispered into her hair and her body relaxed even as her mind took a few more minutes to calm.

"Sorry," she whispered against his chest, cuddling into his warmth. "I know I'm a mess."

"You are not a mess, Miranda," Govek said vehemently, and she sat back to look at him. His expression was an odd mixture, furrowed brow with soft eyes and a grim set mouth.

He continued slowly. "Many injuries cannot be seen, only felt and experienced. That does not mean you are unworthy of care or owe apologies."

"You've had to do so much for me," she insisted, lowering her eyes to the cave floor. Fixing them to the spot where the soft cloak he'd given her met the harsh stone. "And I know I'm never going to be able to pay you back."

"Stop this," he snarled, snapping her back to attention. His expression tightened, and he quickly adjusted her so she was sitting between his legs with her back to his chest.

Much the same way she had been when he'd touched her in the spring. Her thighs clenched.

"I do not want you to *pay me back*. It is my responsibility to offer boons. And in exchange, you allow me to enjoy your company. It is simple." His hands went back to her hair but were a little tighter now. The mild sting felt wonderful. Secure.

"You make this sound so transactional."

"Transactional?"

She tried to turn to face him, but he gripped her shoulders and pressed her firmly into his chest. "Yeah, you know. I give you companionship and you give me stuff in return, but that's not really how relationships work." She paused. "Well, that's not how I want *my* relationships to work. Not that we're in a relationship. I just mean, in general, I want to be on equal footing with my partner."

"What are you trying to say, Miranda?"

She let out a little huff, organizing her thoughts. "It feels . . . dirty to have you giving me physical things in exchange for my company." Especially where sex was concerned. "I don't want you to offer me boons, as you say, expecting I'll spend more time with you."

There was a long pause. Miranda could feel how tense Govek was becoming against her back, but she bit her tongue, determined not to talk over him.

"Then . . . how do I win you?"

Miranda pushed at him until he finally let her turn around. His brows were furrowed, his eyes showed confusion. His jaw was set tight around his upper teeth.

She moved her hands to his jaw, working at the muscles, getting him to lower it back into the right spot. "You've been doing an excellent job of winning me over so far."

His eyes narrowed in obvious confusion, and she almost laughed.

"I like you too, Govek. I would never have begged you to take me with you if I didn't *like* you."

"I was your only option," he muttered, making her snort.

"Arrogant much?" she teased, ruffling his hair and making him blink rapidly. "I figured it out on Earth. I would have figured it out here, too."

"That I believe," he said, the gruff tone turning low and sweet. She smoothed his hair away from his face.

"Your strength is a vision, Miranda. You are a wonder for showing such optimism in the face of your sorrow." Govek leaned close enough to her ear that she could feel the heat of his breath. "Your laugh is like light from the Fades themselves. Your joy reflects in me so strongly it is bliss."

She shuddered out a deep breath, aching and needy.

His lips brushed her ear and his fingertips dragged from her forehead to her nape. "You are breathtaking, Miranda, and all I want in this world is to be allowed the pleasure of continuing to bask in you."

Miranda tripped right over herself, eyes prickling with tears. The depth of his words pulled her into emotions she didn't have a name for.

She forced his hands off her shoulders so she could lean back enough to see his face. Slant her mouth over his.

The sensation of his soft lips contrasting with the harsh touch of his tusks on her cheeks was intoxicating. She craved to make those fangs dig deeper. Get him to open his mouth so she could have a better taste. Use the sting of his sharp teeth to distract her away from the horrors lurking at the corners of her mind.

Govek's growl of pleasure caught her attention, eased her out of her darker urges and back into his warmth and comfort. His hands were so gentle as he threaded his fingers through her hair, like she was so fragile she might snap under his touch. She parted her lips tentatively, wanting to show him she needed more than his gentleness, but unsure how to get it.

He pulled away and the satisfaction in his expression made her realize he had no idea she'd been trying to deepen the kiss.

"Have you made out with someone else before?" Miranda asked, to quell the embarrassing snap of rejection.

"Made out?"

"Kissed." She would have elaborated, but a shake of his head stopped her dead. "What? You've never kissed anyone else?"

He scowled. "No."

Oh, shit. That shouldn't have made her as giddy as it did. "Are you . . . I mean, have you um . . ." He narrowed his eyes, waiting. "Are you a virgin, too?"

He snapped to attention. "I am not. You are?"

Miranda recoiled. Her face was so hot she was certain it could rival the fire. He'd been with another woman? When? What was she like? What did they do together?

"Miranda," he pressed, when she didn't immediately respond.

"What? Oh, yeah. I mean, technically. I haven't had sex with anyone before. You . . . have?"

If he noticed her displeasure, he didn't let on. "Yes. I have. What do you mean by 'technically'?"

She pushed her negative emotions aside and mumbled. "I've gone out on dates and stuff. Made out with a few people."

Govek's deep growl made her shiver.

"You have not had a male between your legs?" he asked, clearly unaffected by the intimate question, even as it threatened to make Miranda disintegrate.

"You had your fingers there."

He rumbled. "That does not count."

She squirmed, heated by his voice. "Will how I answer change things?"

He paused, considering. She held her breath. "No. I will take you regardless. It would only change the ferocity with which I rut you."

She quivered. "Oh, god. Govek you can rut me as ferociously as you want." Hot damn, that's exactly what she wanted from him.

His eyes bulged before he dragged a hand over his face. "Do *not* tempt me, woman. I could cause you great pain from this act."

Miranda became acutely aware of their difference in size. Of the thick lines of muscles in his thighs. Of that massive bulge in his tight underwear. Her thighs clenched, aching.

"I do not wish to harm you, Miranda," he said earnestly before leaning away from her. "And my control is slipping by the moment. You must give me space—"

She raked a hand up his thigh before clasping it around the swell of his cock with no preamble. Miranda was absolutely not going to be giving him space. Her lack of experience made her clumsy, but she gave into her urges, anyway.

She'd never touched a real cock before and she hadn't expected it to be any different from her toys, but Govek was so much hotter, harder. She traced the length to the rim of the head, wishing she was brave enough to get his underwear off and touch him without the barrier.

Govek's breath left him in a brutal hiss that puffed her hair out of her face. He grabbed her wrist so hard it stung, but didn't push her away like she thought he might.

"You aren't that big. I've taken bigger," she said and his once clenched shut eyes burst open, making her realize how insulting that was. "Oh god. Sorry, that's really not what I— you're plenty big. Perfect, actually. Big has always been my preference and—"

"Stop," he begged, moving his hand to clench her fingers. She'd been stroking him and hadn't noticed. He was shaking, and she gulped at the thought that she might have accidentally hurt him. "Just . . . stop. *Please.*"

This was the first time he'd ever told her to be quiet, and she bit the inside of her cheek, searching his face as he yanked his hair.

His breaths were long and heavy before he managed, through the clench of his teeth, "You've taken *bigger*?"

She blinked, fidgeted against his grip. "Do people here not masturbate?"

His cock flexed under her hand and pleasure burst in her stomach.

Govek coughed. His grip tightened, but he still didn't pull her fingers away from his groin. "I . . . I don't fucking *know*. I've been with one female and she did not share her—fuck, Miranda, are you saying that . . . that . . ."

She was so hot she might as well throw herself into the fire at this point. "Oh, come on. It's not that shocking. I'm a twenty-four-year-old woman with a healthy sex drive. And Earth had *lots* of toys to play with."

"Toys?" he choked.

"You know, like . . . fake cocks and stuff. You can't blame a girl for messing around, can you?"

Govek's throat worked in a gulp, but his expression softened, and his eyes closed. A half chuckle, half groan left him, as if he might be trying to imagine it. The tension in her chest eased. "What you describe is considerably more than 'messing around.'"

She giggled, still half embarrassed. "I guess so."

He opened his eyes and raked them down her body. His brow arched showing he was incredulous, but the slight quirk of his lips told her he was impressed.

"Turn around, Miranda."

"Why?" she asked, but he was already forcing her to turn, putting her back to his chest, caging her with his legs like he had in the water. "Why can't I face—"

"Can I remove this?" He plucked at the shirt.

She nodded and focused her eyes on his hands. "Are you going to remove the gloves?"

"No," he almost snapped, and made quick work of the ties on the shirt.

"Why—" Her words cut off in a gasp as he stripped her, making her skin prickle. He tossed the shirt away and pulled her back into him.

He made a thoughtful noise as he traced the edge of the sports bra along the low neckline. Her skin broke out in goosebumps. "How do I remove this?"

It took her a second to realize what he meant. They didn't have stretch fabric on this planet. She pulled the neckline out away from her breasts to demonstrate.

"*Fuck*, woman," Govek snarled into the top of her head. He was tall enough to look over her shoulder and see *everything*. "The Fades must have taken their sweet time rendering you."

She laughed at the compliment, giddy.

Govek's hands moved down from her collarbone to the neckline and stretched it out himself. Taking another long look that made her stomach quiver. He gulped hard and pulled it more.

Embarrassment warred with pleasure and she teased him. "Yeah, I think it could stretch enough to fit you, too."

"That is not what I was thinking, woman."

She grinned at his irritation. "We both know you've been interested since we talked about you wearing a dress."

He half snarled, half laughed, and it broke delicious skitters of pleasure down her spine. "Let me show you what I'm really interested in." His hands dipped under the fabric and cupped both her breasts.

She whimpered, panting as he grazed his leather covered fingers over her nipples, strumming them until she was writhing and flush and had forgotten every teasing comment she could have made.

His hands left her abruptly, and he grabbed the bottom of the bra, stretching it out so he could yank it over her head. He tossed it onto the discarded shirt.

"*Fuck*, Miranda," he said, running his hands down her chest, over her breasts. Flicking and swirling and plucking until she was a trembling ball of need, until her nipples were tingling, and her clit was throbbing.

"*Govek*," she begged, and he finally released her, moving his hands past the flat of her stomach.

He stopped at her shuddering thighs. "I'm going to move you."

"Where?" she gasped, barely able to think as his hands snaked around her hips and cupped under her butt. He kneaded her ass for a second and all the air in her lungs left as tingling bloomed at the base of her spine.

"Here," he grated into her ear as he pulled her into his groin. His cock. She could feel it—thick and hot—but not nearly as intense as she wanted.

"It's not fair," she whined, squirming against him until he hissed harshly and dug his fingers into her thighs to stop her. "I want to see you."

"No."

"Why?"

"Because I need to prepare you."

"Wouldn't being able to see you make preparing me *easier*?"

"No."

"I think it would. And I have more experience with this than you do. It's *my* body. Believe me when I say I've figured out just what I like over the many years I've played around."

"Fuck, woman," he rumbled low, blasting delicious shivers over her flesh. "I am not one of your *toys*."

"Hmm." The thoughtful sound came out like a whimper as his cock twitched. "Maybe, but . . . I'm pretty sure I had a green one."

His breath caught.

"I'd need a good look before I can judge for size, though," she mustered through little gasps.

"Bold words for a fucking *virgin*," he was stripping her of her pants now. Roughly forcing her feet out of the wool and tossing the slacks to join the pile.

"I might be a virgin, but I know what I like," she gasped as he fingered the edge of her panties. "And that's you, Govek."

His breath left him, and his hands stilled.

She reached up to touch his cheek, turning her head to get a good look at his expression, but it was too much of a twist and his grip was too limiting to accomplish it.

So, she simply repeated her words. "I like you, Govek. I—"

Before she could continue, Govek pushed her forward to her knees and yanked her panties off. She gasped as the cold air hit her damp pussy. For a scorching moment, she could feel his eyes on her, raking down her thighs. A thick curse left his lips, so low it made her core pulse. She shivered and craned her neck to see him.

He yanked her back before she could see his face, pulled her into a seated position again with her back tucked tight against his hot chest. She squirmed her hips against his groin and felt the fabric separating them.

Her brow furrowed in impatience. "You aren't going to take your underwear off?"

"Fuck," he breathed, pushing her away. She went back on her knees to give him room, looking over her shoulder so she could watch him strip. His hands were trembling as he reached for the fitted shorts, and in his haste, they tore. Her gut twisted at the repercussions of that even as her body flushed with pleasure that she'd gotten him so crazed.

And then his cock sprang free, and she gasped.

Dear lord almighty, he was huge—long and thick, and wide at the head. He put every one of her toys to absolute shame.

Delicious thrills shot through her. Anticipation and nervousness. Her knees spread a little, as if trying to beckon him.

Govek was frozen, eyes spearing her ass, her wet pussy. He snarled low and covered his face with his hand, squeezing his eyes shut.

"*Fucking Fades, woman.* Sit up." He grabbed her shoulders and forced her back into a seated position.

Then he took up the place at her back again. His heat was so violent it seared up her spine.

"Get back here," he managed between the clench of his teeth. "Right *here.*"

He gripped her ass again and pushed her into his cock. She could feel him between her cheeks, so long the tip was pressing into her lower back.

"*Oh fuck,*" she breathed, squirming on him, unable to help herself. His cock pulsed against her with every movement.

"Stop," he hissed into her ear, which only made the

burning pulse between her legs worse. "Stop or I'll lose my fucking mind, Miranda."

"Isn't that the point?"

He made a strangled sound that was alarmingly close to a whimper, and her body went still. "Govek?"

"Give me . . ." He growled into her ear again, and it only made the ache worse. She shifted her legs, forcing his cock to glide between her ass cheeks. He groaned.

She'd nearly turned so she could see his face, read his expression, when his grip snapped to her shoulders and stopped her. She fought, but he held firm.

"Govek? Why can't I face you?"

"Can't . . . ruin this."

"Ruin it how?" Frustration born from sheer desperation made her stomach clench. He didn't answer, and she tried to turn around again.

"Woman, be *still*," he threatened harshly, "or I will blindfold you."

Oh fuck.

He tensed at her quickened breath and pleading moan. "That was a *threat*, woman."

"Not a very good one." Her voice was so husky she almost didn't recognize it.

He huffed, breathing hard. Working for composure.

Miranda whispered. "Please, Govek?"

He shuddered behind her, his mouth grazing her ear as he rasped, "Fuck, woman. Don't tempt me. I *can't*. I cannot risk . . ."

"You can't risk what?"

He tensed. His hands on her shoulders were trembling. It dawned on her then.

He said he wasn't a virgin, but he'd never been kissed.

He put on gloves before touching her and he'd rather blindfold her than risk her looking at him.

What the fuck had the woman he'd been with done to his self-esteem?

She brought her fingers to his gloved hand and stroked it.

"I know what you are, Govek."

His breathing was ragged, and she took his hand between both of hers. She pressed a kiss to his palm, tasting the leather and wishing it was his skin. "Wearing these won't make me forget you're an orc."

Govek jerked to pull away, and she held firm, stopping his retreat with another lingering kiss. "Even at my back, I can feel how strong you are." She moved to his wrist and nipped at his rapid pulse. "I can't see you, but I can sense you looming over me."

She eased the glove off, following it with her lips and tongue, enjoying the salty taste of him. The warm spicy scent. Govek shuddered. His cock twitched against her back.

"These gloves can't protect me from your claws, Govek. And I don't need them to feel safe with you." She trailed her lips up his fingers and he started huffing out harsh breaths against her ear, heating her tender flesh. "You saved me from the saber cat. Kept me fed. Gave me the clothes off your back. Held me until I was sane when I panicked. Never, not even once, have I ever been afraid of you, Govek."

He groaned and shivered, then buried his nose in her hair and breathed deep. Delicious skitters of pleasure shot down her spine.

Miranda sucked his index finger into her mouth and

laved her tongue right over the nail where his claw was hidden away.

"*Miranda*," he snarled against her neck, his tusks nipped her tender skin right below her pulse. She sucked harder and moved on to the next finger, bathing him with her tongue. She kissed every inch and eased the other glove off while he trembled.

His raw groan burst heat in her stomach and made her core pound with need. She writhed. Bucked her hips back into his rock-hard cock and he choked.

"*Fuck*, woman." He removed his hand from her mouth with a pop, and for a second, she thought he would pull away. That she'd pushed him too far. But then he wrapped his hands around her thighs and ground into her.

Oh, shit. The hard length of him was so hot it made her pant.

He snarled, rumbling smooth, delicious vibration all the way from her toes to the top of her head. "I'm going to touch you now."

CHAPTER

FOURTEEN

GOVEK

Fades be praised. Govek was considering forgiving them.

His hand was damp, tingling, and *raw* with pleasure from Miranda's blissful mouth. Her tongue. She'd fucking licked right over where his claws were hidden without even flinching.

He was losing his blasted mind over her. Nothing could have prepared him for this woman.

He would never be able to let her go. He'd rip the world apart if she tried to leave him. The imprint blazed a brand on his soul.

"*Let me touch you.*" He grated the words into her ear. His gloves were off, and he needed her full permission before going further.

He'd never had this. *Never.*

She shuddered so hard it vibrated his cock and he snarled, incredible pressure squeezing his gut. "Yes," she breathed, and his bare hands grazed down her stomach. Her skin was so blasted soft. He'd never felt anything like it.

"Here," he demanded, bare fingers stopping right above her core. The image of her on her hands and knees flooded his mind, her folds soaked, her thighs glistening in the firelight . . .

She was so wet she was *dripping*. For *him*.

"Anywhere!" His mate cried, raising her hips into his hand. "Touch me anywhere, *please*."

He dipped his fingers low, sliding them between her legs. They glided against her hot folds, slick and easy and *blistering* hot. *Fuck!*

Bliss like he'd never known roared into him. He was touching her full-on, without any covering. He never could have *dreamed*.

"Govek," Miranda moaned. Her head fell back onto his chest, eyes closed in rapture.

"You're so *wet*," he snarled, and it only made her shivering more exquisite. He swirled his fingers around her folds, exploring, learning. There was a little nub at the top and he slid a finger over it.

She jumped, hissing, jerking away from him. "T-too much."

He moved away. Apparently not "*anywhere*." He gritted his teeth, uncertainty dimming his pleasure. She ground her ass against his cock and stars flashed in his vision as he fought for control.

If he didn't get it back, he would do something she didn't like and *ruin* this. She'd reject him, force him out of the cave, refuse to take him back until he brought her enough boons to win her favor.

But there was nothing he could do to get her back. *He had no fucking boons.*

"Govek," she breathed, her voice soft. Gentle. It lacked the rage he'd been expecting. "Like this."

She'd said she didn't want his boons.

She just wanted *him*.

Govek gulped.

She guided his hand to the same position she'd liked in the spring, snaked those two fingers low and into her warm, wet channel.

He fought the need to bellow out his praise.

"*Ooh*," she whimpered, sultry and low, releasing him as he pushed his fingers deeper. He couldn't believe he was being allowed this gift. Couldn't have ever dreamed how hot and wet and *tight* she was.

Govek turned his attention to her reactions, watching her face and the full range of emotions. Her eyes were squeezed shut, her brow was furrowed, and her mouth was open and panting, her limbs twitched and bucked.

Her pleading quickly turned to pleasure tinged moans as he continued to thrust. He curled his fingers into that incredible spot that forced her to babble.

He wanted it to be higher, wanted to drench her in such ecstasy that she never remembered anything but him, wanted to be better than anything she could ever fathom, so she would never leave him or push him away.

"I'm ready," she gasped, grinding her hips into his cock. The sensation skewered through his mind like bolts of delicious, rapture laced lightning. "*Please,* Govek. I want—"

Fades help him. His control was in tatters.

He moved Miranda forward, helping her to get to her

knees, cushioning them with her cloak. The full globe of her ass and thick thighs made him want to shout his thanks to the Fades. She was so wet for him, glistening and sweet and *perfect.*

Her scent was *everywhere.* Maddening and rich.

Govek worked reason into his senses as he slid his palm down her back. She shivered and moaned and arched her back.

Blast, the sight of his monstrously huge hand on her perfect ass ruined him. Her trust was so unfounded. He would split her in two with his force.

His fingers trembled. He was dangerous. Out of control.

"Oh, Govek," Miranda whimpered, causing his angry thoughts to evaporate. She spread her legs. "Please."

She fucking wanted him. *Him.* She'd taken off his gloves. She'd moved his hands. She'd bucked into his touch and gushed all over his fingers.

She was a Fades-given miracle. His miracle. And he would have her.

"Govek."

The sound of his name moaned from her sweet lips thundered through his veins. He gripped her hair, and she tipped her head back, pushing her scalp into his touch instead of trying to struggle away. It seemed she relished his brutal hold and wanted more. Her honey scent flooded the space.

At every turn, his woman cleaved to him. Accepted him. Praised him.

His hand was still tingling and damp from her slick pleasure. The silky strands of her hair engulfed his fingers.

She babbled pleas he couldn't make out.

She wanted him.

Govek gripped his cock and pressed the tip into her folds, wetted it from her dripping, wet center. Spikes of bliss raged as he found her entrance and pushed in. Her body gave slowly. He had to be gentle, but his need was making him crazed and his body shook with the desire to thrust in hard. He quivered with the need to go slow, even as the driving urge to spear her through in one surge seared his gut.

Fucking Fades, she was *tight*. And blistering hot. And his body quaked for more, Running pleasure down his spine and into the soles of his feet.

"W-wait."

He froze, ice gripping his veins. He barely managed words. "Hurting you?"

Fuck, he needed to pull out of her. To retreat. But he couldn't bring himself to do it.

"No- no. It doesn't. It . . . I just . . ."

The tremor in her voice broke him. Fuck, she'd changed her mind. She didn't want him. She would reject him now and he would be hurtled into the depths of misery all over again.

"I don't want to get pregnant."

What? She didn't want to *what?*

"Do you . . . do you have protection, or I mean . . . shit." She shivered and squirmed. The head of his cock was lodged in her, and he felt every blasted shift she made. Devastating bliss spread to his stomach. He wanted to weep.

She whimpered. "I'm not ready to get pregnant yet."

Yet?

"Govek?"

His thoughts spiraled. Yearnings he'd never allowed

himself to consider were making it impossible for him to form words.

"I-If you promise to pull out, we could still . . ."

What was she saying? Pull out? He swallowed hard but finally managed to form a few words. "It takes two ruttings."

"What?"

"Two ruttings," he gasped. She pulsed tight around the tip of his cock and it felt so fucking good. He squeezed his eyes shut. "Two to render pregnancy."

Fades, he knew he needed to offer her more and could not manage words. But he would not force her into this. If she needed an explanation, he would find a way to cool his blood and ease her fear, even if it killed him.

But Miranda relaxed, her body yielding to him. He groaned, rapture dancing up his spine. His head buzzed.

"Okay," her voice was barely a whisper.

Before he could register her acceptance, she pushed her hips back and impaled herself on his cock.

He roared. The sound was deafening. Loud enough to wake the Fades from their slumber and cleave the entire planet in two.

Rapture licked up his gut as he thrust into her. She fucking took him to the base with *ease*, and arched her back, moaning out her ecstasy. She gripped his cock tighter than the gloves she'd stripped him of. Was hotter than the fire before them. She was so wet and slick. Twitching and pulsing.

He lost his senses as he worked his hips. Plunging into her. Rhythmic jerks. Rolling pleasure. He was only aware of Miranda pushing in tandem, spurring him on, forcing him deeper and harder. Her cries drove him daft. He was surrounded by her thick scent, her warmth, her desire.

He braced his hands against the ground, caging her, pressing her torso into her cloak. He buried his nose in her neck, sucking in her sweet scent as he dragged his cock in and out of her wet channel. The pleasure was brutal, almost agony. She was so fucking tight, searing hot, and trembling everywhere. He could feel every twitch and pulse. Her core gripped him so hard he saw stars.

Her honey scent was maddening and thick in his nose. Her body was hot and damp against his.

He picked up the tempo, and she begged for more. Pleaded. Writhed. Her limbs went taut. He dug his fingers into the cave floor, claws piercing deep into the soil and rock. His jaw slacked and trembled. Dripping.

He wanted to bite so *fucking bad*. To taste the salt of her skin. To feel her pulse against his tongue. The need burst from him in a guttural growl that trembled through his stomach.

Miranda let out a harsh cry and her pussy clenched around him, halting his thrusts. She slammed her hot ass into his groin, grinding her soft skin against him as she fell into bliss and exploded with an orgasm.

He gave that to her. *He did.* She was trembling and bucking and bliss wrecked because of *him.* His ecstasy mounted, coiling deep and tight in his stomach. Working spirals of heat up into his throat.

She was fucking screaming his *name.*

Thundering raw bliss exploded as he came and his sight winked out. He was mindless. It was all he could do not to collapse and crush Miranda under him. The pleasure was searing hot, raw, and he wanted more.

He hooked his arm around her soft, trembling thighs so he could hold her tight against his cock, spear her as deep as he could. He wanted her to feel every tiny twitch and pulse. To know what pleasure she was giving him and give it in return.

She ground into him again, arching her back, "Ooh, *yes*, Govek."

Hope speared him as his release tapered. He worked an arm up around her waist, cleaving her to him. She was still trembling and her orgasm was still clenching his cock. Her breathing and heart rate were erratic, but they matched his own.

Govek buried his face in her gorgeous hair and basked in her scent. Imprinted it inside him. Even if she rejected him, he would forever hold it within.

Fades, have mercy. He would do anything they willed if they would whisper his praises into her mind and convince her to stay at his side. Just for a bit longer. For a few more days.

But Miranda came back to her senses far too soon and his stomach plummeted as she shifted away from his embrace. He knew what would come next—swift redressing, harsh complaints, and reproach and disgust in her eyes as she realized who she'd given her body to.

He moved to his side so she could more easily escape, unwilling to keep her prisoner if she wanted to go. She sat up slightly, her movements slow.

She turned to face him and fell back into his embrace.

Govek froze, uncertain as she cuddled his chest. The mingled scent of their mutual release was dizzying. He carefully trailed his fingers through her hair, down her back, over the wonderful curve of her ass.

She was still here. In his arms.

Her lips grazed his chest and his lungs seized. "Can we lay down?"

Lay down? Govek gulped thickly and smoothed her cloak out so her hot flesh wouldn't be chilled on the cold, hard ground. He settled them both down, giving her enough slack she could scooch out of his embrace.

But she didn't. She curled into his frame, her smooth legs twined between his own.

"It's a good thing you like carrying me around," she said, her mouth brushing his flesh with each word. "Because I'm not going to be able to move for a while."

Fuck, he was a beast. "I harmed you. Let me get—"

She laughed. Blessedly *laughed*, and the sound of it choked him. "No, no. The opposite."

The opposite? If he twisted her statement slightly, it sounded like *praise*.

She nestled close. Gentle hands soothing his bare chest. His heart was frantic in his ears as her warmth soaked into his frame.

She wasn't leaving. There were no harsh words. No sharp criticisms. No disgusted looks.

Instead, when Miranda met his eyes, she appeared blissfully content. Sated.

Govek gulped. "Do you . . . require anything?"

She sighed, as if irritated, and his gut pitched. "I should clean up, but I don't want to." Her fingers moved down his cheek to his chest. "Do you want to get up?"

"No." Moving was the last thing he wanted. "Are you hungry?" The fish had gone black and the nearest spring was much too far for him to get more, but he still had some dried meat in his pack.

"Nope," she murmured. The sound was muffled against his chest. Her eyes were closed. "I'm sleepy though."

He relaxed and worked to memorize her perfect face.

Her eyes popped open. "Oh, but are you hungry? You haven't eaten in days."

His chest swelled and a shocked chuckle escaped him. "No, I'm well, Miranda. Orcs can go many days without."

"Doesn't mean you should, though," she whispered, back to being drowsy. Her lips pressed into his chest again and he exhaled every drop of tension he had left.

The fire was high. The night had fallen behind the veil of vines, and he would keep her safe. Slowly, he reached to pull his cloak over the top of her. She didn't reject it. In fact, the added heat relaxed her further.

She pressed her ear to his chest, lids heavy as she listened to the pulse of his heart.

"You will allow me to remain here while you sleep?" He'd never had this joy before. She was bare against his flesh. Vulnerable.

"Of course." She said it as if it was obvious. As if sleeping in a brutal, violent orc's arms after being ruthlessly rutted was fucking *normal*. Even in his clan, conquests returned to Oakwall Village after the rutting.

Only mates stayed.

"You are certain?" he whispered.

She hummed slightly, drowsy, comfortable. Her eyes were shut. Mumbles left her lips, but he couldn't make them out.

"Sleep," he begged, and she blessedly obeyed him. Her lovely features went completely slack.

Govek stayed awake, watching her far too late, but eventually followed her under.

And then he rose far too fucking early.

Miranda had barely moved in the night; her ear was still against his heart. Her breathing was slow, steady, and stirred warmth against his chest.

He gritted his teeth. He did not want to leave her. He wanted to remain here in her embrace until the end of days.

But she would be famished when she awoke, famished and irritable, and his instincts screamed to provide boons to quell that fury.

"I don't want you to offer me boons . . ."

Govek raked a hand over his face. What was he supposed to do then? How could he ensure she would stay with him if she did not want his offerings?

"You've been doing an excellent job of winning me over so far, Govek."

And that was by providing—keeping her safe and well fed.

Govek slowly untangled himself from her, leaving his cloak to keep her snug and warm. The chill in the cave was oppressive. The fire was embers. He gave it a quick stir to get it blazing again. He would not be gone long.

He went to his undergarment and found it ripped beyond easy repair. He had some tools to mend it but would have to do so when he returned to the cave. For now, he put on his slacks, trusting that Miranda would sleep through his absence and wouldn't need them.

In the quiet of early daybreak, Govek abandoned his sleeping mate for the familiarity of the woods. Frost dusted a layer over the fallen leaves outside the vine curtain. The icy scent of incoming snow forced a shiver down his spine and not only because of the cold biting his bare flesh. An oddness gripped the air, a deep thrum unsettling the land. No birds called. He was unable to scent any animals.

There was a storm coming. Likely a blizzard.

His hand grazed over his face, into his hair, and tugged at his scalp until the sting brought clarity. But the clarity it brought made his blood quake, his teeth gnashed, and his claws came out, threatening to slash.

Miranda would not survive a blizzard and he did not have enough provisions to last them through a harsh winter.

Govek circled round the cave entrance in ever-growing arches that took him deeper into the woods. The imprint he carried for Miranda was strong enough he would hear her call even at great distances, but he was loath to go any further than necessary.

The blasted storm had caused every animal to take shelter, forcing his hunt to take longer than he wanted, but not any longer than usual for the season. On a typical winter hunt, he could be gone for a few days, sometimes an entire moon, and only bring back scraps.

It would not be possible for him to sustain Miranda's health.

He would have to fucking return to the Rove Wood Clan.

Blast the Fades for their ruthlessness. Why could they not have dropped her in his lap near Karthoc's forge? Or held off winter long enough for him to get there?

Govek slashed into the bark of a nearby oak, slicing deep through the soft wood with both claws and magic. He cut through with both hands, thrashing his flesh with splinters, gouging harsh and deep until the tree groaned, snapping. It plummeted.

The thunderous boom of it slamming into the ground

rocked him to his core, but did nothing to crack the agony growing in his desperate frame.

Miranda was too weak, Karthoc's forge was too far, and these woods were too fucking perilous for him to guarantee her safety without more provisions.

He would have to return to Rove Wood. To the clansman who wanted him *dead.*

There was no other choice.

Govek dug the wood out from beneath his claws. Some had left scrapes but nothing deep enough to draw blood.

The scent of a small animal speared his senses. The crash had startled it out of its burrow. A rabbit skittered across the leaves, already turned white for winter.

Easy prey.

He gritted his teeth and forced himself to focus on following its tracks. They were frantic and wide at first, then the tracks were closer together as the rabbit slowed, entering the thick underbrush. Govek scented the air to determine where it was cowering and crept around.

Being at Rove Wood did not mean he had to interact with the clan.

Govek took a brief pause in his hunt. The clan had never been warm to his presence. They would likely leave him alone.

Slowly, crouching, Govek silently moved nearer to his prey.

They may not even notice he'd returned at all.

His hand reached through the brush, claws barely extended, magic thrumming behind his eyes. He moved by scent rather than sight. He could smell each rapid breath the tiny creature took. Hear its heart beating in his mind.

Hunting was the only time he ever felt his magic was truly useful.

If the Fades were well with him, he could keep Miranda's existence hidden too. He only needed to gather some supplies, tinctures, and furs for warmth.

The rabbit, sensing danger, thumped its foot in warning, and Govek froze, heart thundering, his claws a hair's breadth from the creature.

He could keep Miranda in his home for a day, perhaps two, and then they could leave Rove Wood together.

It could work. The orcs of Rove Wood wouldn't notice a few meager supplies missing.

They wouldn't expect him to return so soon.

They likely all thought he was dead.

Govek shot his hand forward and snatched up the rabbit so violently it had no chance to even scream. He snapped its neck in a smooth, practiced motion, ending its life swiftly, painlessly.

He looked down at the tiny creature, at how little meat there was. It was the only animal he could scent, and it had only come out of its burrow because he dropped a tree on it. Such luck would likely never touch him again.

Rove Wood was brimming with creatures. The blight wasn't nearly so harsh there. Govek knew where all the best game liked to dwell and where all the best fishing spots were hidden.

How many hunts had he slaved over, only to have his mighty kills scorned and mutilated by novice butchers? How many white rabbits had he caught for Yerina? Dozens? Hundreds? All for the foolish hope that the lavish gown she created with the furs would please her. Earn him her favor.

He'd worked so blasted hard for that woman. For his clan. For his *father.*

A few days, Govek could hunt enough meat and swipe enough supplies from the storeroom. He would have to be quick if he didn't want to be caught. He'd need to mask his scent somehow, but he could handle it.

He would have to. If they got caught . . . if his brethren discovered he was back in Rove Wood with a female . . .

They might take her from him.

His stomach twisted and bile rose in the back of his throat. He could do this. *He had* to. For Miranda.

She called.

He felt her voice rather than heard it. The tangle of it on the wind, like walking through a spider's web. It tingled across his skin each time she spoke, shaking from the imprint's invisible thread which connected them.

Gathering himself, Govek struck out through the woods and back to his mate. His steps were steady but heavy. The rabbit would not be enough for her. His own stomach ached, but he ignored it.

She was still calling when he arrived at the cave. Her frantic tone caused him to hesitate at the vines, trembling as he forced himself to pull them back. He was prepared for her rejection. He'd faced it before with Yerina.

But as he entered the cave, he saw Miranda's expression go from tense to slack with relief at the sight of him. His chest squeezed sharply.

"Where did you go? You should have woken me up I would have gone with you," she said, sitting up on her knees by the fire. She held his cloak tight around her chest for warmth. "Are you okay? Are you hurt?"

Her care for his wellbeing made him ready to collapse into a grateful flood of praise to the Fades. "I am well, Miranda."

"I had a bad nightmare. There was an explosion…"

An explosion? "There is nothing near here that can explode, Miranda. You need not worry." He'd heard of mountains erupting, but it was rare.

But her world had exploded.

Her face was pale, her lip caught in her teeth, her hands wrung. He swallowed hard and could not come up with a way to distract her from her fear. Pull logic back into it. "I knocked down a tree. Perhaps the sound of it worked its way into your dream."

She blinked. "You what?" He saw no reason to repeat himself when he was certain she'd heard him. "You did what? Why? *How*?"

His only response to her peppered questions was to lift his claws to her view.

She paused, her mind working. A snort left her, and he relaxed. "Okay, tough guy. Come here."

His chest warmed with pleasure at her prompting, and he set the rabbit down by the fire. He snagged his pack so he could get her water and food to quell her hunger while he cooked her meal.

He lowered himself in front of her, ready to dig through the pack, but she grasped his hands instead, probing them with her deliciously warm fingers.

She'd gotten dressed while he was gone, in his shirt, her underwear and the cloak he'd made for her. The delicious memory of her naked body had him longing to strip her bare again. She trailed her soft fingertips over his, as if searching for damage.

"Looks like you're okay," she mumbled. "Why did you knock over a tree? Did it insult you?"

He grunted in amusement. Amusement which died away as Miranda rose and placed a chaste kiss to his lips. All warm and sweet against his icy skin. Blast him as a fool. He was dangerously close to tearing off her only set of clothes. By contrast, she lifted his cloak and slung it around his shoulders.

"You're freezing," she murmured, fumbling with the tie at the neck. The warmth of the cloak was nothing compared to her generous actions. Her eyes turned thoughtful, and she said, "Does the air seem . . . different to you?"

He blinked, tipped his head. "What do you mean?"

"I dunno. It's weird, it just feels kinda electrified." His confusion went deeper, and she let out an adorable snort of amusement. "I mean, like there's going to be a thunderstorm soon."

She could sense the incoming storm? "I believe a blizzard will descend upon us soon. That may be what you are sensing."

"A blizzard?" She glanced toward the low fire and pulled her cloak up tighter.

Govek gulped thickly and went to the flames. Using his magic to build them up as he added in a few more logs. "I may need to put the boulder back in place so that the heat inside this cave can be better preserved."

Fuck, would that even be enough? She was wearing literal *scraps*.

And her face went pale. "Is there somewhere else we can go?"

He shook his head. "My cla—*Rove Wood* Clan is still a two-day journey from here. All will be well, Miranda. I will not allow harm to come to you." He'd battle the Fades themselves to keep her hale.

Her throat worked in a swallow, but she nodded.

He finished with the logs and returned to her side. How long did they have before the storm hit? Did he have time to hunt for more supplies? "I may need to go back out. Collect more provisions."

"I should go with you. I can help."

His throat felt tight. "No, Miranda, it is too cold for you."

"But if there isn't much time, then we should both—"

"You can best help by keeping the fire high," he said firmly. "Keeping yourself warm and safe."

"I'm not some fragile butterfly, Govek"—she rose to her feet, ignoring his scowl—"and you can warm me up when we get back."

A low rumble left his throat, and he raked a hand through his hair. He should not rely on her like this, but an extra set of hands *would* be useful with their limited time.

And he was reluctant to part from her again.

"Fine," he muttered, "but you'll wear my cloak too." They'd left her shorts on the rock at the spring the day before so all she had was her underwear and his oversized shirt. He'd give her his pants as well but his underwear were in tatters from his overzealous removal the night before and he wasn't certain what would discomfort her more, his nakedness or the cold.

"Keep it for now. I'll tell you if I get too cold," she insisted and he let out a long sigh laced with resignation. He could carry her if she got too chilled.

Deep in his bones, he felt that delightful thrum of her imprint soothing away his reservations.

He lifted his pack from the ground and gestured for her to follow him out of the cave. "Come then. We'll go to the spring first."

CHAPTER

FIFTEEN

T he woods were uncomfortably quiet.

Miranda hurried to keep up with Govek's quick pace, but the crunching of leaves and twigs under their feet was the only thing that broke the eerie silence. She'd grown accustomed to the constant chatter of birds and her ears ached to hear them again. They'd clearly sensed the descent of the deadly storm charging the air and gone off to hide.

Much like she and Govek should be doing now.

"How far is the spring? We're not going all the way back to the one from yesterday are we?" she asked,

"No, but the closest is still fairly far." Govek didn't break his stride though he did glance back to ensure she was keeping up. "Further than I would like, but there's no game about other than the rabbit I found, so I must try to catch fish. And we need water."

"How long will the blizzard last?" she asked as Govek turned to help her over a huge log he'd just hopped like it was nothing. She took his warm hand in hers, letting it soothe her icy fingers.

"Hard to say. We'll get as much as we can." He helped her to the ground before releasing her. She hurried after him, watching his back become more tense.

She was disquieted at how worried he was, how uncertain. She wished they could go back to last night and forget about the troubles of today. Of yesterday. Everything.

They would be trapped in that cave until the blizzard passed. Her skin broke out into prickling goosebumps and her stomach twisted so hard she thought she might vomit.

"Fades willing, we'll be able to gather enough to last us," he said.

Desperate for a reprieve from her own turmoil, she said, "Tell me about them. The Fades."

Govek glanced at her again, searching her face. "Are you well?"

She gulped hard and forced a nod.

He let out a hum laced with irritation before stopping to hold out his hand. She took it gladly and even though hiking through the woods like this slowed their pace, he didn't complain or let her go.

She gave his hand a thankful squeeze and he let out a contented huff before saying. "There are many legends about the Fades. Most prominently, it is believed that they now sleep deep beneath the surface of our world."

"They're asleep?"

"Supposedly. There is a sylph legend that the Fades have *gone*, that they abandoned this world long ago to seek new ones, but most do not believe so. Most say they grew tired. That they gave their powers to the sentinels, created humans so we could maintain our numbers without their aid, and fell into slumber."

"They created humans to maintain your numbers? So, like . . . to be *breeders* for you?"

"In a way. It is said that when sentinels were created, we were made to be completely individual. The Fades gave us each a specific task, and we did not speak to or work among one another. We had no community. No help other than from the Fades themselves. And when we grew sick or wounded, we perished, and the Fades would create another to replace us."

"Wow, that . . . sounds like a pretty bleak existence." Almost like they were robots.

"Perhaps, but there are no legends about sentinels being discontent with their work or communion. The only mention of it was in a sylph tale that describes the celebration held when humans were finally born. That the sentinels rejoiced upon hearing that the humans would be the ones to maintain our races while we maintained the planet."

Maintain their races? "That makes it sound like humans are supposed to be subservient to the sentinels."

He cast her a dark look. "That is one opinion that sparks the Waking Order's hate of us."

Miranda's throat went tight. "I didn't mean it like that. I'm just trying to understand."

"I know," he said, stroking his thumb over the back of her hand. "I try to understand as well. I often wonder why humans hold the belief that maintaining our communities is less valued than maintaining Faeda."

"It's not that," Miranda looked up to meet his eyes. "It's being told that we *have* to maintain the community. That we *can't* help with the planet instead, even if that's what we prefer. It's not about value, it's about being forced."

Govek hummed in thought, looking up at the colorful canopy. "I hadn't considered this. As I said, sentinels were created with one purpose, and none have questioned that purpose."

"Huh, I can see where there would be a breakdown between the societies then." Miranda gave his hand a squeeze. "A huge misunderstanding where one side wants freedom, and the other does not understand why they would."

Govek paused in his stride to search her face before finally saying, "You make it sound so simple. And yet I cannot see any solution. Humans cannot commune with the Fades. They were not created with the ability to do so. And no amount of slaughter and war is going to change that fact."

Miranda swallowed hard.

Govek looked away. "The disconnect between our races only becomes greater with every passing season. Because humans reject the role the Fades have given, nature *itself* is rejected. It causes the blight that you saw on the saber cat. It causes the plants to wither. Harvests are less plentiful. Winter comes on too soon and stays too long."

His bitter tone sent a spiral of dread down Miranda's spine. "What are you going to do?"

"There is nothing sentinels can do. The members of the Waking Order are the ones who do not see that the rejection of their purpose is the cause of our world's demise. In order to end the blight, they must end the war. At the very least, they must cease the slaughter of sentinel kind and allow us to return to the task of maintaining Faeda in peace." He looked back into her eyes, the resignation heavy in his face. "But I do not see that happening fast enough. It may already be too late. I often wonder if the Fades must wake to make this world whole again."

A dark thought crossed Miranda's mind. "But . . . what if the sylph's were right? What if the Fades aren't on this planet anymore?"

What if they had gone to Earth? Put humans on her planet too?

And humans destroyed Earth, just a little faster than they were destroying Faeda.

She shook her head. The Fades might not even be real.

Glancing up into Govek's face had her instantly regretting her words. He looked stricken and defeated. Pale and shaky. Throat tight, teeth tucked high.

She reached up to stroke at his firm jaw, forcing it down again.

He took a deep breath, relaxing. "It is unlikely that the Fades abandoned us, otherwise how would communion still work? Besides, sylph seers often divined elaborate, impossible things that hold no true bearing on our world."

"Seers? Like people who can see the future?" she asked as he began to walk again, pulling her along quickly. She tried to ignore how dark the sky was becoming. An icy breeze was starting up.

"That is one of their gifts, yes." Govek's warm hand was firm and bracing as she kept the brisk pace. "A few seers are born to every generation of each sentinel race. They can communicate directly with the Fades and the Fades tell them of the future, warn them of calamities so that they can advise our leaders."

"I see." She was out of breath already.

"The orcs have many seers. They work directly under our overlord, our overarching leader, whose keep is located at the far other end of our world. Very few seers ever come to this side of the mountains. The only one I know of works under my cousin, Warlord Karthoc."

"I . . . see," Miranda said, wondering where exactly he was going with this.

"He . . . may be able to divine why you were brought to our world."

She lost her battle with maintaining pace and forced him to stop so she could search his face. "Really? He could really tell me that?"

Govek nodded. "The seer knows many things. His knowledge comes directly from the Fades themselves. And I believe . . . I believe they brought you here for a reason."

"For a reason? What reason?" Her stomach twisted painfully.

"You've shed more light on your kind in this one conversation than I have learned in an entire lifetime, Miranda," Govek said slowly.

She lost all her breath. "You . . . you think I can do something to mend things between your race and the humans? You think I could stop the *war*?" This was inconceivable. It was all she could do to fight the war going on in her mind.

"No, Miranda," Govek said swiftly. "You are but a single being. I only meant that if there *was* a purpose for you being brought to our world, perhaps the seer in my cousin's clan could divine it."

Miranda let this sink in for a long moment as they continued onward. She watched the muscles in Govek's back contract in a sure rhythm, felt the stinging chill from the ever-growing wind. The growing dim as the clouds grew thicker pulled her thoughts inward, reflecting.

She had not been able to save Earth, hadn't even been given the chance to *try*.

But . . . what if she could try to save this one? What if she *could* save Faeda? At least in some small way. Even the thought was overwhelming, threatening to suck her down into the murky depths where reality was distorted by *hope*.

"Miranda?"

Govek's sharp tone dragged her out of her thoughts, and she managed to gain back her composure. "I'm fine, just . . . thinking. About the seer. What else could he tell me?"

"The seer's power is immeasurable. If the Fades will it, he will know."

She sucked a breath in through her teeth. "How far do we have to travel to reach him?"

"Too far." Govek said slowly and her heart sank. "The lands through which we must travel to reach my cousin at Baelrok Forge are war torn and ravaged."

"Oh." Who was she kidding? They might not even survive the incoming blizzard.

"We . . . will have to stop for supplies at my *former* clan."

She blinked. "Stop for supplies at your . . . you mean the Rove one you mentioned?"

"Yes," he said firmly, picking up the pace, making it obvious he didn't want to give more details.

But she wanted them. "That's your clan? That's where you are from?"

Silence bloomed between them, broken only by the sound of their feet crunching in the leaves and the tension rising at the back of Miranda's throat.

"It is not my clan any longer. My original plan was to join Warlord Karthoc at his forge."

His original plan. Miranda felt sick.

"You mean to war?"

God, was she going to lose him, too?

Govek tightened his grip on her hand. "My cousin's forge has many positions. I will try to convince him to put me in one that does not see much battle."

That was *not* reassuring. "Govek, couldn't we just talk to the seer and then leave? Go somewhere that isn't in the middle of the war? Or send him a message to meet us somewhere safe?"

She felt him gulp as his lower jaw began to tuck up, but he didn't speak.

"What about Rove Wood Clan? Are they at war too?" How long did she have to brace herself before being thrust into turmoil all over again?

"We are *not* staying at Rove Wood Clan," Govek said with such vehemence that she felt a zing of anxiety spike down her spine. "We will not even interact with any of them."

Miranda gulped hard. "Are they cruel? Would they hurt us? Me?"

"I would not allow them to harm you." His tone was adamant enough that she relaxed. His pace slowed. "And they wouldn't wish too. Human women are precious."

"But what about you? Would they try to hurt you?"

A tremor passed through him. Rippling over his skin and darkening his eyes.

Her heart skittered to a halt. What horrors were haunting his past? What secrets about this Rove Wood Clan was he keeping from her?

Before she could start quizzing him, he said, "We will stay away from them. We need only stay long enough to gather enough supplies for the journey to Baelrok Forge. Ideally, they will not even realize we are there."

"Uh . . . how are we going to get supplies from them without talking to them?"

Govek shot her a tense look, and that was all she needed.

"Okay, so let me get this straight. We are about to sneak into a clan of orcs who don't like you, *steal* from them, and then head off to another clan that's in the middle of a war?" Miranda's stomach felt like a pit. She didn't know if she wanted to laugh or cry.

"That is . . . basically it."

"That's a really bad plan, Govek," Miranda said, head spinning. "We're *not* doing that."

"There is no other option, Miranda."

"There's always another option. What about another clan?"

"The other clans are also at war and are not nearly as fortified as Baelrok Forge."

"How about just in the woods, then? We've been doing fine so far."

"You will not survive, Miranda. The winter is too harsh."

"I've survived worse, believe me."

"Miranda."

"Govek."

He sighed raggedly, releasing her to rake a hand through his hair. Stepping away. Closing off.

She'd pushed him too far, and she'd about reached her limit too. Her head was pounding, and the chilly wind was growing oppressive. It matched the storm brewing behind Govek's brooding eyes.

She bridged the small gap between them and wrapped herself around his arm, forcing him to relax under her again. "Let's talk about this later. We'll have plenty of time while we're trapped in the blizzard."

Her words made him tense further, so she rushed in. "For that and a lot of other much more fun things." She stroked a hand down his chest, along his stomach, and he let out a low groan when she stopped. "I guess we can't, though, can we?"

"What?" His voice was strained.

She tried to hide a grin at his telling expression, like a child who'd just gotten his new toy swiped. "You said having sex twice would get me pregnant. Obviously, we can do *other* things."

Her mind was swimming with all the delicious ideas rolling around in her head.

"It has to be twice in *succession*. Within the same quarter of the day." He stepped a little closer. "What are these *other things*?"

She cast him a mischievous look. "So, you mean to say there's a time limit on it? How does that work?"

"It is the Fades design, Miranda. That is all I know," he said quietly, drawing her near. She could feel his warmth as he loomed above her, his eyes sparkling. "Now, tell me what other things you want to do."

"Aw . . ." she said, walking her fingers back up his chest. His breath left him in a rush, and she could feel his heartbeat thumping hard and fast against her fingertips. "But if I tell you, then that ruins the fun of exploring on your own."

His low growl hummed delicious pleasure up her spine and her hands made it up to his shoulder, pulling him down for a kiss.

Only to be blasted by a harsh, bitter wind.

And not just *wind*, sticks and leaves, too. They smacked her cheeks, and yanked at her hair. The trees whistled with the force and branches bowed around them. Swirling.

They both looked to the sky and found the clouds rippling in odd patterns. The coloring was strange too, casting the forest in an eerie glow.

"We have to go back." Govek tugged her in the direction of the cave. "Hurry."

He set a punishing pace, but Miranda did not utter a word of complaint. The electric feel to the air was growing thick. The wind was picking up, and a distant thud radiated through the trees sounding far too much like the thud of Govek knocking over the tree.

Then there was another. And another.

"G-Govek," Miranda barely managed. Her lungs were burning, and her legs screamed from the effort of hiking at such a fast clip.

The wind bellowed and howled, bending the trees all around them. She watched them sway and go still.

But the roaring sound of the wind didn't stop.

"Hurry!" Govek demanded, but she couldn't keep up. Her knees threatened to give way and her lungs burned, ready to explode, and she tripped on a root.

Govek snatched her up, gripped her wrists tight and yanked her into his body as they were pelted with more leaves and twigs. They stung as they scraped her skin and ruthlessly yanked at her hair, spiraling around them like a cyclone.

"G-Govek, this wind is . . ."

She broke off as he yanked her up into his arms and sprinted, hurtling through the woods at a speed that was unimaginable.

The sky was so dark it felt like night. She had no idea how Govek was able to see. She clung about his neck, chest pressed into his so she could not tell the difference between her hammering heart and his. The booming sound of trees falling made her bones quake.

"What is going on?" she screamed over the roaring of the wind and the crashing limbs. One landed directly in front of them, making her shriek, and Govek leaped over it without pause. For a moment, all she could do was stare in awe at the destruction. The forest bending to the sudden storm's mighty force.

"It's just there!" Govek bellowed, and she craned her neck to see that the cave was close already. Damn, he was *fast*.

And shelter was *right there*.

Chaos surrounded them. Closing in. And in the distance, between the barren trees and whipping leaves she saw—

Trees buckled and were ripped from the ground. Shrubs were stripped bare of their leaves in an instant. The leaves swirled, careening in upward circles so fast they were blurs of red and yellow.

"T-tornado?" Miranda gasped, hardly able to breathe. The air was thick with grime now. The wind was too fast, and her lungs felt as if they were going to burst.

"Fucking Fades wrath!" Govek snarled as they burst into the cave. Darkness surrounded them, and through the doorway, she could see the swirling destruction closing in, coming nearer.

"Govek, we have to—" Miranda screamed, only to have the sound cut short by a massive crack. A shattering quake. The wind spiraled around them, snuffing out the fire and sending embers flying through the air.

Govek dropped her to the ground and jerked toward the opening of the cave, clearly about to try to bar it shut with the boulder, only to freeze, eyes going wide.

Miranda looked too, barely making out the mouth of the cave now that there was so much ash and dust in the air. The sparks had all gone out, and the darkness swallowed her up.

Another crack had her eyes straining to see what was going on. Where the next threat was.

She found it in an instant.

The front wall of the cave was *breaking apart.*

From the entry, jagged cracks were forming, splintering like lightning through the cliff side. The rock rumbled and groaned, buckling under the force, spraying more dust into the raging air.

It was going to come down.

They would be crushed.

"We have to get out of here!" Miranda screamed at the top of her lungs and the sound was almost swallowed up. The roaring of the wind was so powerful. Her eyes streamed from the soot, her throat burned, and her tongue tasted of grime.

"We're going to be buried alive!" Miranda gripped Govek's arm, giving him a shake. He wasn't moving. Wasn't even looking at the exit. They had to run *now,* or they wouldn't make it.

The first rocks began to fall, booming against the howling wind.

Govek gripped her, forcing her against his chest and

curled around to protect her, dragging her deeper into the cave.

Deeper into the darkness.

No! *No!* She couldn't!

She couldn't go back into the dark.

They would be buried alive.

Just like she had been on Earth.

"Let me go!" she wailed, but she could barely hear herself over the shattering of rock.

"Miranda!" Govek roared, managing to get her attention. He pushed her back against the cave wall and she broke into coughing sobs. He pressed his palms against it, right next to her head, caging her in.

A glow surrounded her, and she gasped. Craning her neck, she found that the cave wall had lit up, creating bright white patterns and geometric shapes.

Deliberate carvings.

"Govek, what—" She broke off in another cough. She couldn't get enough air. There was too much dust. Her lungs felt like they would explode if she took one more breath.

"Cover your mouth with your shirt!" Govek screamed, the latter half of his words cut off by more crackling pops. She looked behind him and could barely make out the crumbling wall. The light faded.

They were running out of time.

Govek gripped the shirt for her and brought it up around her mouth. "*Breathe*, Miranda!"

His hands went back to the wall as he roared, "You must be silent when we enter!"

"W-what?"

"It is the goblins realm." He bellowed so loud her bones shook and she could still barely make it out over the roaring of wind and cracking of rocks. "If they find we have broken in they will . . ."

Will what?

One look at his face and she knew it would *not* be good.

But it was either this or be *crushed to death.*

Govek's eyes squeezed shut in concentration, and the glowing patterns bloomed to life again.

Booms shook the cave as boulders fell. Miranda gripped Govek for support as the ground beneath her feet bucked and trembled.

She looked back and the magical glow had illuminated the darkness. Bringing the rock face into horrible focus.

It was rippling and buckling like *water.* It was mere seconds from crumbling down.

Right on top of them.

"Govek!" she screamed just as stale air slammed into her back.

Goosebumps broke out all along her arms.

Her stomach twisted.

Her forehead broke out into a cold sweat.

Her wide eyes glanced back, and her heart seemed to stop.

The darkness of the tunnel was pure *agony* to behold. It hooked its claws into her mind, dragging her out of her sanity and into the icy churning depths of *dread.*

"No! Govek, *no!*"

Her voice did not sound like her own.

"We must!" He somehow managed over the thundering booms of boulders falling all around them.

"I can't go in there! I can't!" she wailed, clawing at his hands. "God, let me go."

She would not survive this. *She was going to die.*

Alone.

In the dark.

He gripped her hard under the arms and dragged her into the black.

Into the vault.

Into the vent.

Where she should still be.

On Earth.

She should not have been able to escape that burning death.

She hadn't.

She was there again.

Burning alive in the vent.

She couldn't get out.

She felt herself shattering. Glittering pieces of her sanity rained down around her.

Her mind fractured apart.

She was *gone*.

To Be Continued . . .

MIRANDA AND GOVEK'S STORY CONTINUES IN

The Orc Outcast's Mate
Releasing July 2024

They all say he's dangerous, but she can't stay away.

Miranda is desperate to protect her family, and that includes Govek.

Rove Wood Clan holds nothing but contempt for the male who saved her. The picture they paint of Govek is in such stark contrast to the sweet and caring orc she knows that Miranda can hardly believe they are the same person.

But defending Govek against his brethren's hostility isn't the only fight brewing on the horizon. Desperate to discover what happened to the children from the daycare she worked at on Earth, Miranda seeks out the orc seer, a male with immeasurable magic power beyond her imagining.

However, the seer wants absolutely nothing to do with her and Govek warns that pushing the issue could lead to disaster.

Convinced that this is what she was brought to Faeda to do, Miranda presses forward against all warnings. She will seek the truth at all costs.

Even if that cost is losing the male she's grown to adore.

Govek is desperate to keep Miranda, no matter the cost.

Miranda's light and warmth has lit up Govek's entire world and now it all threatens to come crumbling down.

Between his brethren's constant attempts to separate Miranda from him, and the orc Warlords untimely visit, Govek finds himself torn between staying silent, and telling his new woman the truth of his vile past. Miranda is bound to discover his atrocities eventually, but he fears telling her his secrets will result in her abandoning him.

He *cannot* let that happen. He's been stuck in dreaded darkness for his entire miserable life, and she is his light. A pillar of support, ready and willing to speak out for him against his clan's scorn.

But now she's determined to speak with the seer, a male whose magic instantly rendered Miranda unconscious after a single shake of the hand. Govek can feel in his marrow that the consequences of using the seer's power will be severe.

But so too would the consequences of trying to stop her.

Govek cannot lose her, or he will *lose his mind.*

WANT MORE NOW?

The Orc Gardener's Strawberry

How many vases does an orc really need?

Growing up in Oakwall village meant Savili was no stranger to the attentions of orcs… in a trading capacity.

But when her sister's merciless prank reveals the true intentions of the orc gardener she's been trading with, haggling for strawberries becomes the very last thing on her mind.

Savili must quickly decide if she's going to keep to eating his strawberries… or let him eat *her*.

Iytier has been pursuing Savili for the better part of a year, and she barely knows he exists.

He's turned his hands black trying to impress her with his magic, only to ruin what little progress he'd made when he's tricked into finding her in a *very* compromising position.

With the prospect of losing his chance to win her teetering on the horizon, Iytier must finally drop his reservations and convince Savili to drop hers as well.

The Orc Gardeners Strawberry is a cute and spicy short story focusing on the love between two characters featured in book three of the Orc Mates of Faeda series, with brief appearances from both Govek and Tavggol!

Follow this QR Code or go to https://www.aurorawintersromance.com/rm1-sign-up to subscribe to my newsletter and you'll get this free short story!

LET'S KEEP IN TOUCH!

Sign up for my newsletter on my website,
www.AuroraWintersRomance.com
or follow me on Instagram @aurorawinters.romance.

ACKNOWLEDGMENTS

Thank you SO much for reading my debut novel! I truly never thought I would ever put one of my books out into the world and I'm grateful to every one of you who took the time to read The Orc Outcast's Conquest. If you want to go above and beyond you could head on over to Amazon and leave a review.

So many people helped to make this book possible. A special thank you to my husband for supporting me through all my writing woes and keeping the house afloat during crunch times when I was spending every spare moment at my keyboard.

To Daisy, who spent countless hours helping me edit the books and giving feedback on video calls. The books would not be what they are today without your advice!

To Lacey Braziel at Lacey Braziel Edits for your expert line and copy editing. And to Cassie Weaver at Weaver Way Author Services for your awesome beta reading, proofreading, and formatting. You both rock!

And once again, thank you to all of my readers! I appreciate every single one of you.

ABOUT AURORA WINTERS

Growing up in the Pacific Northwest meant many rainy days spent on indoor activities and from a young age one of my favorites has been creative writing. I was penning monster romance stories in high school between classes before I even realized it was a genre and still have many of those original drafts. (Which will never, ever see the light of day again because they are truly cringe worthy!)

It was only recently that my writing grew from a personal hobby into a dream of publishing. When I'm not obsessing over my writing, I can be found wandering through the woods with my daughter and husband, taking pictures of pretty leaves, and throwing sticks for my little dog, Dash.

Let's keep in touch! Join my newsletter at www.AuroraWintersRomance.com.

www.ingramcontent.com/pod-product-compliance
Lightning Source LLC
Chambersburg PA
CBHW022126310726
48972CB00007B/2216